AF556245

# POST-HARVEST ROTS OF FRUITS

*By*

**Sumia Fatima**

*M.Sc., Ph.D.*

*Head, Department of Botany*

*Aurangabad College of Women*

*Aurangabad–431 001*

**Zafar Javeed**

*M.Sc., Ph.D.*

*Director*

*Rural India Research Laboratory*

*Aurangabad–431 001*

**Avinash Ade**

*M.Sc., Ph.D.*

*Lecturer*

*Department of Botany*

*Dr. Babasaheb Ambedkar*

*Marathwada University*

*Aurangabad–431 004*

**DISCOVERY PUBLISHING HOUSE**

**NEW DELHI-110002**

*Published by:*

**Tilak Wasan**

**DISCOVERY PUBLISHING HOUSE PVT. LTD.**
4383/4B, Ansari Road, Darya Ganj
New Delhi-110 002 (India)
*Phone* : +91-11-23279245, 23253475, 43596065
*E-mail* : discoverypublishinghouse@gmail.com
sales@discoverypublishinggroup.com
*web* : www.discoverypublishinggroup.com

***First Edition:* 2006**

***Reprinted:* 2020**

**ISBN: 978-81-8356-177-8**

**Post-harvest Rots of Fruits**



*Printed at:*
Infinity Imaging Systems
Delhi

# Preface

While teaching plant pathology as a lecturer, I felt a need of a book on the diseases of fruits which occurs during storage. Much literature has been published on diseases of cereals, pulses, oil seeds and garden plants etc. The present book is an effort to inculcate and popularise this branch of pathology among the persons who are concerned this discipline. This includes an updated revised of the reported post-harvest fruit diseases. This will be highly beneficial to the students, teachers and researchers to make them familiar with the type of post-harvest rots of fruits and sources of its cause. Definitely this will divert a plant pathologist to think off a neglected branch of post-harvest diseases of fruits.

**Authors**

# Contents

# Introduction

Popular trends and dietary changes have greatly increased the importance of fruits and vegetables. The nutritionists also placed fruits and green vegetables on the top because, fruits contain all essential ingredients required for good health. Fruits and vegetables provide essential minerals, vitamins and dietary fibers. Fruits contain 50-90 per cent moisture. The prize of fruit is due to their flavours, aroma and taste. Being soft textured, fruits are highly sensitive to the exogenous agencies such as fungi and bacteria etc. that affects the quality of fruit and causes loss of fruit seller. The diseases of harvested fruits due to fungal or bacterial pathogen cause quality degradation of fruits which are called post-harvest diseases.

The market pathology is a special branch of pathology, which is firstly emphasised by Powell (1906). Steven and Stevens (1952) defined market pathology is a branch of pathology related to fungal disease occur during transit and storage.

In fact, the branch of market pathology initiated due to improper, handling of harvested fruits or dormant storage organs, unfavourable environment of storehouse or godowns and mechanical injuries caused during harvest and transportation. Packing material must be soft and smooth. Packing must not be creating any pressure on fruits otherwise there are possibilities to occur cracks and injuries to the fruit. It is highly difficult to control saprophytic fungi which are grown on injured fruits in tropical regions of the world.

In case of post-harvest diseases, disintegration and decay of the edible pulp of the fruits occur. This type of event in nature is normal for the fruits. Any change in the fruit after harvest affect the quality of fruits. The psysiological and morphological change in the harvested fruits is also caused due to the activity of micro-organism especially due to growth of saprophytic fungi and bacteria. The micro-organism (fungi and bacteria) causes considerable damage, if the environment is favourable during transportation, storage and marketing process.

Some of the pathogenic fungi attack fruits at immature stage and some other infect tissue of overripe fruits. Some of the pathogens infect fruits in the field before harvest, but severe rot occurs due to the same pathogen in godowns during storage period.

Thc fungal forms responsible for post-harvest diseases of fruits are arbitrarily divided into three types. The first type infects the fruits at the early stage of maturity and the disease develops before climacteric sets in. The second type of fungal forms infects the fruit only after ripening has started. In presence of favourable environment, both these types of fungi can invade the fruit tissue and causes degradation of fruits at physical and biochemical level, and cause considerable loss. The third type of fungi infects the peel of the fruits causing superficial blemishes and generally do not invade the deeper tissues of the fruits. This causes little loss of fruits.

Susceptibility of fruits to the attack of fungi vary according to site, season, variety, mechanical injuries and harvesting conditions as well as by post-harvest treatments and storage conditions (Derhyshriue and Shipway 1978, Dennis, 1983).

Many of the storage disease of fruits and vegetables are initiated by the concentration of fungal spores present in the air of fruit shops itself.

The following forms of fungi isolated from the air at godowns of fruits are *Penicillium sp. Aspergillus niger, A. flavus, Rhizopus, Alternaria, Curvularia, Cladosporium, Trichothecium*. Sumbali and Mehrotra (1981) isolated highest percentage of *Penicillium sp.* from the air of godowns which were found to cause green and blue mould diseases of orange and amla.

In the fruit market of Aurangabad, it has recorded that 30-40 per cent of the fruits get injured during transportation and 20-25 per cent loss of fruits was due to poor storage systems.

In India, 2.95 million hectare area occupied by the fruit crop (Neeta Sharma and Mashkoor Alam, 1998).

## Post-Harvest Losses

Major loss of harvested fruits is caused due to fungi. The diseases caused before harvest of fruit also responsible for degradation of quality and cost of fruits in market. Post-harvest loss of fruits may be due to susceptibility of fruits to the fungal growth. The physiology and morphology of fruit is also responsible for susceptibility of fruit to post-harvest rot diseases. The soft skinned fruits are more susceptible than tough skinned fruits. The soft skinned fruits require careful handling. The injured fruits are highly susceptible than uninjured ones in all types of fruits. Post-harvest diseases of fruit alter the physiology of fruits and reduce its market value. Not only the handling of fruits by wholesalers is responsible for injuries and post-harvest rots of fruits but many times we purchase fruits and store in fridge or in kitchen. Generally we never eat it immediately. We eat as we wish; it has observed that the fruits get infected due to long term storage at home and we throw out the rotted fruits in dust bins. This activity of man increases the air and soil borne inoculum of post-harvest fungi responsible for rot diseases of fruits. So that our activities must be against, the post-harvests losses of fruits.

All the stages of harvested fruits are susceptible for post-harvest fungi, if the environment is favourable for development of fungal growth. The loss of money due to post-harvest disease varies between and within markets.

The modern agricultural systems of harvesting fruits are also responsible for mechanical injuries to the fruits during harvest.

The quality of fruit lowers due to wide range of factors. The humidity and temperature are responsible for psysiological changes in healthy fruits. Both these factors also influence the establishment of pathogen on injured fruits.

The value of the fruit directly related with quality of the fruit. A slight change in the quality of fruits causes economical loss. The quality of fruit depends on size, shape, flavour, and colour, absence of skin rashes, injuries, taste and texture. Physiological changes occur in the infected fruits due to biochemical interaction of pathogen and host. The physiological disorders of fruits also caused due to adverse environmental factors. Low as well as very high temperature causes direct loss of water from fruits; due to this the fruits become more susceptible to fungal decay. High humidity reduces dehydration of fruits but also influence growth of fungi. In presence of high humid conditions, there greater and greater loss of fruits caused due to fungi. However, the factors like handling of fruits, temperature and humidity during harvest period, mechanical injury, the time of harvest, type of storehouse, age of fruit during harvest, injuries caused before and after infection, packing system during transportation, type of packing material, storage period, environment of godowns, distance of transportation, type of road might affect the behaviour of fruit. The post-harvest diseases can be reduced by the use of proper packing material, packing techniques and careful handling of fruits. In the fruit market of Aurangabad, the apples are sold in markets which are coated with waxy substance to avoid moisture loss of fruits that increases the shelf life of fruits. The thin polythin bags are also used as packing material that reduces dehydration of fruits and helps to extend shelf life of fruits and spread of microflora from one fruit to others in a single package.

## Life of Fruits

The process of reaching of any fruit from fruit tree to the consumer's mouth is a very complex process. It passes through number of steps i.e. harvesting, handling collection, packing, transportation, storage and marketing. All these steps are closely related with self-life of fruits.

Harvesting of fruits must be on proper maturity of fruits. Immediately after harvest, within a certain short-time interval the stem ends of the fruits remains wet hence, we have to take precaution to avoid fungal attack to the stem end region. Hence, to avoid infection to the fruit, avoid keeping the harvested fruits on soil surface in the same field. After few minutes of harvest, the stem ends secrete sticky watery substance and dry up, that forms a protective wall on the cut ends of fruit. The dried sticky walls of stem ends of fruits restrict the growth of many fungi causing post-harvest diseases.

In the Pesticides and Plant Protection Research Laboratory of Aurangabad College for Women, Aurangabad, it has observed that the stem end of immediately harvested fruit of mango inoculated with spore suspension of *Aspergillus niger* and another set of three mango fruits inoculated by the same fungal suspension 6 hours after harvest. The results were that the fruits inoculated immediately after harvest were shown infection on $3^{rd}$ day of inoculation period and the another set of fruits which were inoculated 6 hours after harvest were also get infected after 8 days of inoculation period. Hence the immediately harvested fruits should be protected from contaminated containers and contact of soil surface to avoid post-harvest rot diseases.

The environmental factors during harvesting period also affect the disease developments especially in injured fruits. Moderate temperature and humid atmosphere is favourable for the growth and development of most of the post-harvest rot causing fungi. The type of variety of fruit tree also affect intensity of disease development in the field as well as in storehouses. The plantation system of plants of different cultivars is different. In India, harvesting of fruits is dependent on the decision of cultivativer who is untrained. This factor also causes loss of fruits.

Handling of fruits is very important factor. The major loss of harvested fruits takes place due to improper handling during and after harvest. In India the loss of fruits is very great because, the people working in fruit field are less or non-educated and non-trained.

The soft skinned fruits like Banana, Strawberry, Aalubukhara, Sapota, Amla, Grapes and Papaya etc. are required very careful handling. The fruit skin being very soft, get easily punctured due to any mechanical agency during harvesting and packing systems. The smallest injury to the fruit is responsible for post-harvest rots of fruits. In fact, it is very difficult to restrict the rot of inured fruits. Careful handling of fruits can avoid post-harvest losses at maximum extent.

In rural areas, the Indian farmer who maintain fruit crop fields, but after harvest of the fruits, he collect all the fruits in the same field on soil surface up to the time of packing. Even the large fruit growers have no facilities of collection of fruits immediately after harvest. They do not sort healthy and injured fruits and collect all the fruit without packing in bullock cart and take to the market for sale. This system of marketing favours the development and spread of fungal flora causing post-harvest diseases. Transportation of unpacked fruits gets injured easily. Injured fruits are extremely susceptible for post-harvest rots. Transportation of unpacked fruits causes about 60 per cent loss of fruits due to skin injuries observed in soft walled fruits. When the fruits are to be transported to the long distance markets are only packed in cartoons or in waste leaves or soft paper cuttings to avoid injuries. Considerable amount of fruits also get injured due to hard packing material.

Packing material of soft fruits should always be soft and sterile. It is very essential to leave space between fruits in container during packing and the gap between the fruits should be filled with sterile, soft, smooth, packing material. Packing of fruits should be done in the field during harvest to avoid prolonged exposure to severe temperature and contamination. Packing should be uniform and attractive. Disease intensity and inoculum of post-harvest fungi can be reduced if fruit harvesters and packers are trained and expert.

## Spread of Inoculum

The survey report indicates that majority of fruit sellers are non-educated, they do not have any idea about the fungi, infection and spread of disease. Practical observation of Aurangabad fruit market is that whenever the loaded fruit reach the market, the owners collect the fruits on soil surface, then start sorting of injured, infected and healthy ones. They store all healthy fruits in godowns and remaining injured and infected ones throw out on the road side or dustbins nearby without any precaution where the fungi get more favourable environment and grow extensively. The air around the market becomes highly contaminated with fungal flora, which is also indirectly responsible for post-harvest rot of stored fruits. Spread of post-harvest fungi is also due to poor sanitary techniques followed by the godown owners. Non-aerated godown environment is also responsible for development and spread of post-harvest diseases of fruits.

The dominant saprophytic fungal forms responsible for fruit rot diseases in Aurangabad market are *Aspergillus*, *Rhizopus* and *Penicillin sp.* which can grow on wide range of fruits and causes degradation of quality of fruits. The saprophytic forms of fungi like *Aspergillus* and *Rhizopus* enter the fruit through injured areas. Some are specific that penetrate the epidermis by mechanical pressure or secrete enzymes which degrade the wall of host epidermis and enters the fruit.

The general, etiology of the diseases in concerned, the infection by fungal flora often initiates while the fruits are still on trees example: Anthracnose pathogens that attacks all the aerial parts of the tree. Usually such infections remain inside the fruits that develop during ripening of fruits in storehouse. On the other hand the mechanical injuries during harvest cause huge loss of fruits due to growth of post-harvest fungi. Because most of the saprophytic fungi and bacteria make their entry in to the fruit through these injuries and causes rot of the fruits. The spores produced on diseased fruit concentrate the atmosphere of the godowns, and fruit markets, particularly fruit shops and serve as source of inoculum to the flesh fruits. Sumbali and Badyal (1991) studied the occurrence of airborne fungal flora causing post-harvest rot of fruits.

The air-borne fungi have a definite relationship with the diseases of harvested fruits.

Spoilage due to post-harvest diseases is maximum during the high humidity and optimum temperature periods. Such an environment is highly favourable for well establishment of fungi causing post-harvest rots.

Post-harvest diseases of fruits are also non parasitic or physiological in origin. The non-parasitic post-harvest rot of fruits also caused due to adverse environmental factors i.e. low or high temperature, very low oxygen or due to freezing injury, or chemical injuries. In Aurangabad market the losses due to post-harvest diseases are more because of absence of adequate and proper godowns. Alam and Khan (1983) investigated losses of fruits due to post-harvest infection of fungi at different places. The rainy season i.e. June to August is more favourable for post-harvest rot of fungi in Aurangabad district. Post-harvest loss of fruits depends on type of fruit and environmental factors. Percentage of loss of fruits varies according to the whether, intensity of inoculum and storage conditions. Longer duration of transportation of fruits is responsible for highest pick point of loss due to post-harvest fungi. The saprophytic fungi like Aspergillus sp. Fusarium sp. Rhizopus etc. are not host specific. Such fungi can attack most of the injured fruits of any type hence causes huge loss of fruits during storage and transportation. The host specific fungi like, Penicillium sp. on orange, Colletotrichum sp. on mango also causes severe post-harvest diseases of fruits. The soft skinned fruits like papaya, tomato, grapes, sapota, plum etc. require immediate transportation after harvest. We can restrict the diseases of soft skinned fruits for some extent by avoiding contact of fruits on soil during harvest. The rough skinned fruits like Pomegranate, pineapple and bael etc. does not get infected immediately during transportation because of tough skin which consists of different types of fungi restricting chemicals. Only the injured rough skinned fruits can get infected easily. These fruits have long self-life due to presence of fungitoxic substances in the skin. In developed countries cold storehouses are there for storage of fruits. The refrigerated or fruits stored at cold store godown, require immediate transportation in-comparison to freshly harvested fruits. The refrigerated fruits become more susceptible because of biochemical changes in it or might be due to loss of immunity towards pathogens. The heavy loss of fruit takes place when the fruits are transported in large bulk without packing in van or lory or in bullock cart. The loosely packed fruits get injured during transportation on which saprophytic fungi start growing. If the fruit is rotted only 5-10 or 15-20 per cent, even though we could not eat the remaining uninfected part, as a precautions we think that, the toxic compounds might be spread in the pulp of infected fruit. With the help of external morphology, we can not understand whether the fruit showing 10-15 per cent rot might be safe for eating or not, we discard all such rotted fruits. Hence the post-hārvest diseases of fruits are an important aspect for all plant pathologist of the world. Fungal forms are the main source of post-harvest rot of fruits in market. The quality of fruits directly affects the fruit value. The loss of quality of fruits is also caused due to poor marketing systems. Many of the psysiological disorders are due to oxygen deficiency. Quantitative losses are mainly caused due to improper storage and marketing way. The activities of human being during harvesting, selection of packing material, transportation and storage are related with quantitative losses of fruits. The saprophytic fungi grow within a short period on injured fruits and develop very fast, that become difficult to control and there is no value for injured fruits in market. Rough handling of fruits by workers is only due to lack of knowledge of market standards to them. Hence, it is essential that, all the workers should be pre-trained about the market standards of the fruits to avoid fruit losses due to post harvest diseases.

## Role of Temperature and Relative Humidity on Post-harvest Diseases of Fruits

The storage temperature and relative humidity of the post-harvest environment have an important role in promoting fungal advancement and decay. Wells (1962) and Lentz and Venden Beng (1971) have emphasised the importance of temperature and relative humidity in post-harvest diseases. According to Harvey (1978), very high humilities generally favour the growth of many fruit rot fungi and subsequent reduction in losses of market fruits. Wardlaw (1935) pointed out that the temperature and humidity plays and important role in determining the type of decay caused by fungi in storage. Choudasy (1935), Bhargave et al. (1965), Kaul (1984), Narania and Reddy (1978). Prasad and Bilgrami (1973). Singh (1975) and Tandon (1967) have emphasised the role of temperature and humidity on fruit rots caused by different fungi in mango, banana, guava, apple, lemons, litchi and pomegranate, respectively. Low temperatures are inhibitory for fungal advancement in fruit tissue. All the post-harvest rots caused by fungi fall to show significant amount of rotting for 2-4 days at room temperature 28° ± 2°C. All the post-harvest rot fungi fail to show appreciable amount of rotting at temperature of 10 and 15°C. However, penicillium citrinum on Amla (Emblica officinale) show considerable rotting even at 10°C (Diwakar, et al. 1986).

In general, the saprophytic fungi grow extensively and cause severe rot of fruits between temperature 25 and 30°C (Diwakar, et al. 1986; Bhargave, et al. 1965; Prasad and Bilgrami, 1973; Singh, 1975; Shrivastavas and Tandon, 1968; Shrivastava, et al. 1965).

Harvey and Pentzet, (1960); Harvey, et al. (1972) advocated the necessity of storage of different fruits at lower temperatures is preferably around 10°C. Such a lower temperature minimises the loss due to fungal invasion. It delays the advent of senescence and consequent decrease in resistance in fruits and it also slows down the rate of advancement of the pathogen and subsequent decay of the fruits.

Prasad and Bilgramy (1973) reported the importance and role of temperature and humidity in case of fruit rot diseases. Temperature and humidity have profound influence on the rate of decay of fruits in storage. Temperature and humidity have direct effect on the parasite and pre-disposing effect on the host. In general, large numbers of fungi were found to be associated with the diseases of fruits, but only few of them were found to be responsible for post-harvest rots of fruits. Each pathogen has its separate range of temperature for different rot causing organising vary. Bhargava et al. (1965) observed that the magnitude of loss suffered by the fruits of mango, banana and guava due to the infections caused by different fungi showed a considerable variation in different parts of the country and temperature is one of the important factors responsible for such variation. Effect of temperature and humidity on the decay of mango, banana, papaya, guava, citrus, pomegranate and certain other tropical and subtropical fruits have been studied by some workers (Dastur, 1921; Rose. et. al. 1943; Choudhary, 1955; Singh, et al. 1963; Williamson, 1964, Shrivastava. et. al. 1965; Bhargava, et al. 1965; Shrivastaga. 1968; Tandon and Singh, 1969). The influence of the environment, particularly temperature and humidity plays a very important part in determining the nature and activity of the micro flora. Thus factors not have only direct influence on the growth of the fungi, but they can also appreciably affect fungal advancement indirectly by increasing or decreasing the resistance of the host. Storage of fruits at lower temperatures may prevent rapid losses, but a change from very low temperature (10°C) to the room temperature resulted in severe infections within a few days, this obviously indicates that the tissues of the fruits may become weak and susceptible during storage even at low temperature, but the infection is delayed because the pathogen is not able to grow at that temperature (Prasad and Bilgrami, 1973). Initial studies have shown that even under cultural conditions, the rot causing fungi was not able to grow 10°C. Even above this temperature, they accomplished a very limited growth upto 20°C. Tandon (1969) has recommended the storage of mango, papaya, banana an guava fruits within a temperature range of 10 to 15°C. Wardlaw and Leonard (1936); Chema, et. al. (1939), Karmakar and Joshi (1940) as well as Mukherjee (1961) have recommended the storage of mangoes at 10°C temperature to avoid fungal infection during storage. At room temperature 33 ± 2°C fruits get spoiled within 5-6 days.

Kanwar, et al. (1973) reported maximum rot of pomegranate due to growth of Rhizaopus arrhizus at 30°C temperature.

Misra and Singh (1962) studied the effect of temperature and humidity on disease development in Bihar. The optimum temperature for conidial germination of Gloeosporium musarum is 30°C. The maximum number of conidia germinates within four hours at 30°C temperature and the germ tube also showed a faster rate of growth. The optimum temperature for Gloeosporium rot of banana is 30-53°C. The Gloeosporium rot of banana arrested during cold as well as hot and dry months (Thakur and Mishra, 1964).

Maximum rot of banana by Botryodipodia theobromae occurs at 25°C temperature (Williamson and Tandon (1966). Per cent germination of spores of B. theobromae was more at 25°C temperature observed under laboratory conditions.

**Table 1.1: Per cent rot of different fruits at different temperatures**

| Host | Pathogen | Days of incubation | Per cent rotting Temperature in °C | | | | | |
|---|---|---|---|---|---|---|---|---|
| | | | 10°C | 15°C | 25°C | 28±2 | 33±2°C | |
| 1. Pomegranate | Rhizopus asrhizus | 10 | 33 | 33 | 100 | 100 | – | Kanwar et al. (1973) |
| 2. Litchi | Asperfillus flavus | 6 | 13.9 | 22.4 | – | – | 100 | Diwakar et. al. (1986) |
| | A. nidulaus | 6 | – | 4.1 | 35.2 | – | 80.3 | |
| | A. niger | 6 | – | 8.3 | 89.6 | – | 100% | |
| | A. quadrilineatus | 6 | – | – | 28.4 | – | 67.8 | |
| | A. Variecolor | 6 | – | 6.8 | 64.8 | – | 100% | |
| | Botryodiploidia theobromae | 6 | – | 6.0 | 64.8 | – | 96.7 | |
| | Colletotriclum gloeosporioides | 6 | – | 5.2 | 39.6 | – | 87.2 | |
| | Cylindrocarpon tonkinense | 6 | – | 5.8 | 47.8 | – | 90.8 | |
| | Pestalotia sp. | 6 | – | – | 22.9 | – | 54.6 | |
| 3. Amla | Penicillium citrinum | 8 | 24.4 | 38.6 | – | 64.2 | – | Prasad & Bilgrami (1973) |
| 4. Grape | Greeneria uvicola | 8 | 6.2 | 171 | – | 32.4 | – | |
| | Pestalotiopsis mangifera | 8 | 8.4 | 13.0 | – | 17.6 | – | |
| | Drechslora howaiiense | 8 | 3.4 | 11.2 | – | 46.6 | – | |
| 5. Ber | Fusarium decemcellulare | 8 | – | 16.4 | – | 23.6 | – | |
| | Atternaria atternata | 8 | 3.6 | 13.5 | – | 25.8 | – | |
| 6. Jambolan | Pestalotiopsis palmasum | 8 | 4.6 | 11.2 | – | 18.6 | – | |
| | Fusarium semitectum | 8 | – | 8.2 | – | 14.6 | – | |
| 7. Mango | Rhizopus arrlizaus | 20 | – | – | 100% | – | | Thakur (1972) |
| 8. Grape | Phamopais viticola | 12 | – | – | 100% | 100% | | Shea (1961) |

**Table 1.2: Favourable storage temperature for maximum rot development in fruits**

| Sl. No. | Fruit | Pathogen | Temp. | Reference |
|---|---|---|---|---|
| 01 | Banana | Botryodiplodia theobromae | 25-30°C | |
| 02 | Citrus | Penicillium italicum<br>P. digitatum | –<br>25°C | Baker, et al. (1940) |
| 03 | Mango | Colletotrichum gloeosporioids<br>Aspergillus niger<br>Rhizopus arrhizus<br>Pestalaia mango ferea | 30°C<br>35°C<br>30°C<br>20°C | Shrivastava (1968)<br>Patil and Pathak (1993)<br>Panday and Mohammad |
| 04 | Apple | Glomerella cingulata<br>Rhizepus stolonifen<br>r. arrhizus<br>Botryodiplodia | 27°C<br>36°C<br>25°C<br>25- | (1974-75)<br>Noe and Starkey (1982)<br>Luepschenetal (1971) |
| 05 | Mango | theobraae<br>Phomopsis viticola | 28°C<br>30- | Tandon (1967) |
| 06 | Grapes | Gloeosporium musarum | 53°C<br>30°C | Shea (1961) |
| 07 | Musa | Botry. Theobramax | | Misra and Singh (1962) |
| 08 | Sapota | | | Tandon (1967) |

Tandon (1967) studied the effect of temperature on tropical fruits. He found that sapota fruits stored at low temperature (10°C) did not develop any rot for eight days. Shrivastava (1966) working with tropical fruits found that the sapota fruits inoculated with Botryodiploidia theobromae escaped rotting for ten years at 10°C. Effect of temperature on the fungal decay of sapota fruits was studied by Tandon (1967). In case of Pestalotia sapotae, there was no rot at 10 and 15°C temperature upto eight days of incubation but in case of Botryodiplodia theobromae 2.8 per cent rot was observed after eight days at 15°C temperature. Sapota fruits infected with P. sapotae did not show any rot at 20°C upto 4$^{th}$ day of incubation period but after eight days of incubation, the rot was 20 per cent. The loss of fruits increases between 25-35°C temperature. The B. theobromae is capable of causing rot at 15°C temperature. The maximum rot of sapota due to B. theobromae takes place at 30°C.

Humidity has also profound influence on post-harvest rot of fruits in storage. The humidity has direct effect on fungal forms and hosts. Effects of humidity on the rot development of certain fruits has been investigated by many workers mentioned below.

The post-harvest diseases of fruits are most severe when the relative humidity will be between 90 and 100 per cent (Tandon and Singh, 1969). During moist environmental conditions, the affected fruits get covered with huge sporulation of fungi. As the humidity decreases, the severity of infection decline sharply. In general, it was observed that higher the relative humidity, the greater will be the area destroyed by rotting. Therefore humidity is one of the important factor for heavy infection and spread of the post-harvest disease. A number of workers including Dastur, (1921); Park, (1930); Chowdhary, (1950); Sattar and Hafiz (1953); Chowdhary, (1955); Shrivastava, (1968). Tandon and Singh (1969) also found maximum disease development in case of various fruits between 90 and 100 per cent relative humidity. Diwakar, et. al. (1986) studied the effects of different humidity levels on rotting of fruits. The rotting was most severe when the relative humidity was between 80 and 100 per cent. According to Diwakar, greater the humidity level more will be the severity of post-harvest rot of fruits. Severe spoilage of fruits occurs between the humidity range 80-100 per cent. Earlier observations showed that the high humidity is essential for spore germination and penetration of the host tissue. The Pestalotiopsis mangiferae on grapes, Alternaria alternata on ber preferred 90 per cent humidity rather than 100 per cent. Tandon and Srivastava (1968) and Prasad and Bilgrami (1973) also found maximum disease development in guava and litchi fruits respectively at 90 per cent humidity. Narania and Reddy (1978) recorded maximum citrus fruit spoilage due to Fusarium oxysporium at 90 and 100 per cent humidity.

Thakur (1972) observed prevalence of soft rot in various fruits and vegetables at all humidity levels by a species of Rhizopus. Post-harvest rot of amla by Penicillium citrinum and Greeneria uvicola rot of grapes is high at all humidity levels (Diwakar, 1986).

Kanwar et al. (1973) reported that the Rhizopus arrhizus causes maximum soft rot of pomegranate at 80 per cent of relative humidity.

Misra and Singh (1962) observed germination of conidia of Gloeosporium musarum within the range of 85.7—100 per cent relative humidity.

Post-harvest rot of banana caused by Botryodiploidia theobromae increases due to increase in per cent humidity (Williamson and Tandon, 1986).

# 2

# Post-harvest Diseases of Guava

The injured guava gets infected by fungal forms during transit and storage. The common fungal farms grow on injured fruits in godowns during storage are Alternaria, Aspergillus, Colletotrichum, Curvularia, Fusarium, Monilia, Penicillium, Pestalotia, Phytopthora, Rhizopus and Syncephalastrum sp.

**Table 2.1: The post-harvest rot diseases of guava**

| *Sl. No.* | *Fungus* | *Place* | *Reference* |
|---|---|---|---|
| *1* | *2* | *3* | *4* |
| 01 | Alternaria alternata | Allahabad, UP | Shrivastava, et al. (1964) |
| 02 | A. chartarum | Calcutta (W.B.) | Saha (1945) |
| 03 | Aspergillus sp. (A. nanus, A. phoenicis) (A. niger, A. pasasitica,) | Calcutta (W.B.) | Thom and Raper (1945) |
| 04 | Colletotrichum gloeosporioides | Common | Khanna and Chandra (1976) |
| 05 | Curvularia Lunata | Allahabad (U.P.) | Kapoor (1970 b) |
| 06 | C. tuberculata | Allahabad (U.P.) | Kapoor (190b) |
| 07 | Fusarium oxysporium | Common | Shrivastava, et al. (1964) |
| 08 | Macrophama allahabadensis | Allahabad | Kapoor (1970 b) |

*(Table Contd...)*

| 1 | 2 | 3 | 4 |
|---|---|---|---|
| 09 | Monilia sitophila | Clacutta (W.B.) | Saha (1945) |
| 10 | Penicillium decumbens | Calcutta (W.B.) | Saha (1945) |
| 11 | Pestalotia olivacea | Karnal Haryana | Dhingra and Mehrotra (1980) |
| 12 | Phoma psidii | – | Tandon (1967) |
| 13 | Macrophomina allahabadensis | – | Kapoor and Tandon (1970) |
| 14 | Phytopthora nicotianae | – | Dastur (1947) |
| 15 | Pestalotiopsis psidii | – | Tandon (1967) |
| 16 | Botryodiploidia theobromae | Udaipur | Patel and Pathak (1993) |
| 17 | Diplodia natalensis | – | Tandon (1967) |
| 18 | Phytopthora parasitica | – | Sohi (1983) |

## 1. Aspergillus Rots of Guava

The little injury to the fruit invites the post-harvest fungi. The Aspergillus rot of guava is very common among injured fruits. The Aspergillus rot initiate as a water soaked lesion. The lesions are of brown colour and have an irregular margin. The spot increases with age of fruit. The spots get depressed in the centre. In severe cases, black moldy growth of Aspergillus niger appears on the infected surface of the fruit. The whole fruit looks black because of conidial heads of the fungus within few days of infection. Lal, et al. (1980) reported 20-25 per cent loss of fruits during transit and storage. The Aspergillus nanus, A. phoenicis, A. parasitica, A. flavus and A. awamori also responsible for rot disease of guava, Thom and Raper (1945).

### Cause

Aspergillus niger van Tiegh.

### Control

1. Krishnaiah, et al. (1985) tried post harvest protection of guava fruits using Decca food grade fruit coatings. The coating at 0.04 ml/100 gm fruits can control most of the

spoilage fungi like Penicillium, Colletotrichum, Curvularia, Fusarium, Glomerella, Phytapthora, Pestulotia, Gloeosporium etc.

2. A Careful handling of fruits can reduce disease intensity.

3. Dry and ventilated storehouse minimises inoculum of post-harvest fungi.

## 2. Post-harvest Rot of Guava due to Colletotrichum sp.

Generally the Colletotrichum psidii associated with pre-harvested fruits. It forms dark brown spots on fruits. Initially the spots remain small and circular. In storage, the dark brown spot increases in size and the pulp under the infected spot becomes hard. The oblong to elliptical spots of variable size develop more prominently on upper surface of fruit. Lesion show black concentric rings. The spots frequently coalesce and involve, most of the portion of fruit resulting in drying and death of the tissue (Khanna and Chandra, 1976).

### Cause

The rot is caused by Colletotrichum gloeosporioides (Penz) Sacc. (Khanna and Chandra, 1976).

### Control

1. Protection against Colletotrichum gloeosporioides is done by dipping fruits of guava in 50 ppm Aretan for two minutes (Khanna and Chandra, 1976).

2. Gamma radiation (100 kr) also controls the post-harvest rot of guava (Gupta and Chatrath, 1973).

3. Sharma, et al. (1984) treated guava fruits with Thiobendazole and Aureofungin against Colletotrichum rot.

4. Hot water treatment of infected fruits at 50°C for 5 min. has been found to reduce disease severity by Majumdar and Pathak (1991).

## 3. Post-harvest Rot of Guava due to Botryodiploidia sp.

The post-harvest losses of guava fruits caused due to Botryodiploidia reported by Patel and Pathak (1993) to the tune of Rs. 56,016 in 1989.

### Symptoms

The Botryodiploidia attack the harvested fruits during transportation and storage show brownish discoloration at the stem-end region that gradually increase to rest of the fruit in the wavy manner. In severe cases, all infected fruit surface get covered by numerous pycnidial bodies. The condiomata of Botryodiploidia theobromae are pycnidial, conidia at first aseptate, hyaline, when mature becoming one separate, brown, longitudinally straight, 20-30 X 10-15 um, extruded from the pycnidia in clearly visible, black powdery mass.

Hundred per cent humidity and temperature between 25-30°C is favourable for the establishment Botryodiploidia theobromae (Patel and Pathak, 1995).

### Cause

Botryodiploidia theobromae (Kehri and Chandra, 1986).

### Control

1. The hot water treatment combined with the vapor heat treatment provides adequate control of post-harvest rot of Botryodiploidia theobromae.
2. Healthy, uninjured fruits can resist the pathogen B. theobromae.
3. Collection and destruction of unhealthy fruits can reduce intensity of Botryodiploidia rot of guava.
4. Avoid injury to the fruits.
5. One per cent arsenic oxide completely inhibits the germination of spores of B. theobromae in vitro studies.
6. Hot water treatment to immediately harvested fruits at 50°C temperature for 5 minutes reduces intensity of post-harvested rot of guava during storage.

### 4. Post-harvest Rot of Guava due to Phytopthora sp.

Sohi, 1983 reported Phytopthora rot of guava during rainy season in Rajastan and Karnataka. The rotted fruits emit a characteristic odour. The fungus affects the green fruits. The infected fruits possess circular brownish spots. The infection on the fruit develops further in storage and results into appreciable damage.

### Cause

The rot is caused by Phytoptoora parasitica Dast. var. nicotianae Sohi, (1983). The coenocytic hyphae produces many terminal sporangia which contain biflagellate, kidney shaped Zoospores. Zoospores cause secondary infection in storehouses.

### Control

1. Spray of Benlate at 10 ppm concentration two month before harvest is effective against the disease.
2. Monthly spray of Diathane Z-78 at the concentrations of 0.2 per cent during the months of June to November, gives control of disease.

## 5. Post-harvest Rot of Guava by Thielaviopsis State of Ceratocystis Paradoxa

Lal, et al. (1980) reported a new post-harvest rot of guava caused by Thielaviopsis state of Ceratocystis paradoxa (Dade) C. which is responsible for huge damage to harvested mature fruits. This disease is also called soft rot. It is very common in the markets of Allahabad and Baroda.

### Symptoms

Infected fruits shows circular water soaked areas with white mycelial growth in the centre which later changes to black in colour due to production of black conidia at the centre of the spot. Heavily infected fruit get covered with dark coloured fungal mycelia and spores. The fruit changes its shape due to rot disease. Finally the flesh of the fruit turns black, soft and pulpy. The infected fruit can be easily identified due to dirty foul odour emitted by the fruits.

### Control

1. Bavistin 500 ppm and Difolatan 1000 ppm used as post-inoculation treatment (Lal et al., 1982). The disease incidence is influenced by interactions of temperature, humidity, inoculum potential and physiological state of fruit during storage.
2. Deep rice straw in waters containing salt for 10 minute and dry in bright sunlight and use as a packing material to control of pathogen for some extent.

3. Discard infected fruits immediately.
4. Avoid any mechanical ınjury to the fruit during harvest, transit. storage and marketing.
5. Clean and well aerated godowns play an important role in reducing disease intensity caused due to post-harvest fungi.

## 6. Myrothecium Rot of Guava

The Myrothecium rot of guava is firstly reported by Rai, et al. (1980). This rot disease is also known as soft rot disease. It infects the fruits before harvest and that develops after harvest of fruits. The infected fruit shows slightly sunken, small circular, olive gray patches which gradually increase in size. The spots get covered with huge growth of white woolly mycelium with dark green viscid spore mass. The pathogen remains restricted to the infected region. Dissemination of spore occurs when fruits are collected in a container.

### Cause

Myrothecium roridum Tode ex. Fr. The mycelium is wooly with numerous greenish spores.

### Control

1. Careful removal and destruction of infected fruit during harvest control disease for same extent.
2. Myrothecium rot is not a major post-harvest disease. Only the infected fruits before harvest show symptoms that affected the quality and cost of fruit.
3. Use of resistant varieties can avoid Myrothecium rot of guava.

## 7. Physalospora Rots of Guava

Rai et al. (1982) firstly reported Physalosporea rot of the guava from the fruit market of Allahabad.

### Symptoms

The infected fruits show circular brown coloured water soaked lesions which later changes to dark brown in colour.

The spots gradually advance towards stem end. The whole fruit get infected within 7-8 days.

### Cause

The casual organism is Physalospora psidii Steven and Peirce.

## 8. Rhizopus Rots of Guava

The fully mature and injured fruits are more susceptible for the soft rot caused by Rhizopus nigricans Ehrenberg (Tandon, 1967).

### Symptoms

The infected fruits show water soaked lesions which are circular in outline. The rot increases day by day and the affected area get covered with mycelial mat of the fungus. The rot caused by the Rhizopus nigricans is soft and watery in nature. High humidity and moderate temperature is most favourable for the soft rot of guava.

### Cause

Rhizopus nigricans Ehrenb.

### Control

1. Do not store injured fruits with healthy, non-injured fruits.
2. Try to avoid injury to the fruit during harvest.
3. Collect and destroy infected fruits immediately.
4. Proper ventilation of storehouse is essential for control of Rhizopus rot of fruits.
5. Dipping of harvested fruits in hot water at 50°C temperature check the Rhizopus rot of guava.

## 9. Post-harvest Rot of Guava due to Phoma sp.

Post-harvest rot of guava due to Phoma sp. is common in store-houses. Phoma psidii hydrolyse the entire sucrose content of guava fruit within six days.

### Symptoms

The circular spots are formed on the surface of infected fruits. Generally the spots might be brown in colour. The centre of spot gradually gets depressed. The margin of spot may be water soaked.

The spots ooze out cream coloured pycnidiospores. Pycnidia are minute dot like structures.

### Cause

The casual organism is Phoma psidii P. Henn. (Tandon, 1967). The conidiomata of Phoma species are pycnidial, thin walled, conidiogenesis enteroblastic. phialidic. The conidia are typically aseptate and hyaline.

### Control

1. Discard infected fruits immediately.
2. Pre-harvest treatment with 1000 ppm of Tecto-40 controls 60 per cent disease (Bhargava and Singh. 1994).
3. Careful handling of fruits is essential.
4. Singh & Bhargava (1977) effectively controlled Phoma rot of guava by dipping fruits in Benomyl 300 ppm for 5 minutes.

## 10. Post-harvest Rot of Guava due to Fusarium sp.

Severe losses were reported by Fusarium oxysporium var. psidi (Shrivastava et. al. 1964); Rai (1982) isolated the pathogen from the infected fruits in Allahabad.

### Cause

Fusarium oxysporum (Schlecht. Ex Fr.) Emend. Snyd. & Hans.

### Symptoms

The characteristic symptoms of the disease are yellowing and browning of the fruits. The injured fruits get attracted immediately. Rarely the infected fruit shows white cottony growth of fungus. The infected patches become water soaked. The pulp becomes lucid. Infected fruits emit foul odour.

### Control

1. Handle the fruits carefully during harvest and storage to avoid mechanical injury to the fruit.
2. It is impossible to control Fusarium rot after infection to the fruit.

3. Avoid keeping harvested fruits on soil surface.
4. Packing of fruits must be comfortable with soft material.
5. Pre-harvest spray of thiophanate methyl is recommended by Ansar, et al. (1994) for the control of post-harvest rots of guava.
6. Addition of Trichoderma harzianum and Arachniotus sp. in soils amended with wheat straw is tried by some pathologist for the control of Fusarium rot of guava.

# Post-harvest Diseases of Papaya *(Carica Papaya L.)*

Post-harvest rot of papaya caused due to various fungal flora. The fungal forms of major importance are Macrophomina, Rhizopus and Phomopsis sp. These are commonly associated with storage rot of papaya fruits.

**Table 3.1: Post-harvest rots of papaya**

| *Sr. No.* | *Fungal forms* | *Geography* | *Reference* |
|---|---|---|---|
| *1* | *2* | *3* | *4* |
| 01 | Ascochyta caricae | Burnihal (Assam) | Chowdhary (1950) |
| 02 | Botryodiploidia theobromae | Gwalior (M.P.) | Tandon (1967); Prasad and Verma (1970) |
| 03 | Colletotrichum gloeosporioides | Jabalpur (M.P.) | Ratnam and Verma (1967) |
| 04 | Fusarium sp. | Jabalpur (M.P.) | Ratnam and Verma (1967) |
| 05 | Rhizopus nigricans | Bhusawal | Srivastava, et al. (1964) |
| 06 | Rhizopus arrhizus R. stolanifer | Jobner, Rajasthan Bhusawal | Goyal, et al. (1971) Pathak, et al. (1976) |
| 07 | Selerotium rolfsii | Poona Maharashtra | Uppal, et al. (1935) |
| 08 | Macrophomina phaseolina | Common | Kapur and Chohan (1968) |

*(Table Contd...)*

| *1* | *2* | *3* | *4* |
|---|---|---|---|
| 09 | Rhizopus stolonifer | Common | Pathak, et al. (1976) |
| 10 | Phomopsis caricae-Papayae | Jabalpur | Dhingra and Khare (1971) |
| 11 | Fusarium solani | Common | Shukla, et al. (1978) |
| 12 | F. roseum | Common | Tandon (1967) |
| 13 | F. moniliforme | Common | Arya, et al. (1986) |
| 14 | F. oxysporium | Common | Lal & Arya (1982) |
| 15. | Colletotrichum capsici | Maharashtra, Kanpur | Lal, et. al. (1979) |
| 16 | C. papayae | Akola | Wangikar & Rout (1972) |
| 17 | C. dematium | Hyd. Karachi | Solangi & Malik, (1971) |
| 18 | Gloeosporium papayae | Allahabad | Tandon (1967) |
| 19 | Ulocladium chartarum | – | Lal, et. al. (1984) |
| 20 | Hyalodendron sp. | – | Arya, et. al. (1986) |
| 21 | Memnoniella echinata | Allahabad | Rai, et. al. (1982) |
| 22 | Alternaria tenuis | Patna, Bihar | Tandon (1967) |
| 23 | Chaetomium globosum | – | Prasad & Verma (1970) |
| 24 | Curvularia lunata | Bhusawal | Tandon (1967) |
| 25 | Nigrospora oryzae | Bhagalpur, Patna | Prasad & Verma (1970) |
| 26 | Trihothecium roseum | – | Tandon (1967) |
| 27 | Phytopthora parasitica | – | Tandon (1967) |
| 28 | Cladosporium gloeosporioides | Allahabad | Tandon & Verma (1964) |
| 29 | Alternaria tenuis | Patna | Prasad & Verma (1970) |
| 30 | Aspergillus flavus | | Tandon (1967) |

*(Table Contd...)*

| 1 | 2 | 3 | 4 |
|---|---|---|---|
| 31 | A. fumigatus | | Tandon (1967) |
| 32 | A. nidulans | | Tandon (1967) |
| 33 | A. niger | | Tandon (1967) |
| 34 | A. terreus | | Tandon (1967) |
| 35 | Cladosporium cucumerinum | | Tandon (1967) |
| 36 | Corynospora cassiicola | Jabalpur | Hasija (1962a) |
| 37 | Penicillium implicatum | | Prasad & Verma (1970) |

## 1. Post-harvest Rot of Papaya due to Macrophomina

Heavy loss of fruits caused by Macrophomina phaseoli (Maubl.) Ashby. Kapur and Chohan (1968) reported 5-20 per cent losses in Punjab during summer.

### Symptoms

Affected fruits possess small water soaked spots on fruit surface. Gradually the spots increase in size and become deeper and sunken causing rotting of inner tissues. In severe cases, small sclerotia develop on these spots. Pulp of fruit becomes brownish-black in colour, due to growth of fungal mycelium. The fully mature ripen fruits are more susceptible. Raw and small sized fruits are less susceptible to rot disease. Kapoor and Chohan, 1968 reported that the M. phasceoli could cause infection to injured as well as uninjured fruits under humid conditions. The injured fruit shows rot symptoms earlier than the uninjured fruits. The disease is also known as charcoal rot.

### Cause

The charcoal rot is caused by Macrophomina phaseoli Tassi (Goid). The pycnidia are brown, thick walled, canidia aseptate, hyaline, cylindrical to fusiform measuring 16-24 x 5-9 nm. The fungus produces sclerotia which are black, smooth and hard upto 1 mm in diameter. The fungus is very common in tropical areas (Ashby, 1927). Maximum rot of fruit occurs at 30°C temperature and 100 per cent humidity (Kapoor and Chohan, 1974 b).

# "Photographic Representation of Post-harvest Rots of Fruits"

Aspergillus Rot of Mango

Rhizopus Rot of Mango

Fusarium Rot of Papaya

Colletotrichum Rot of Papaya

Penicillium Rot of Amla

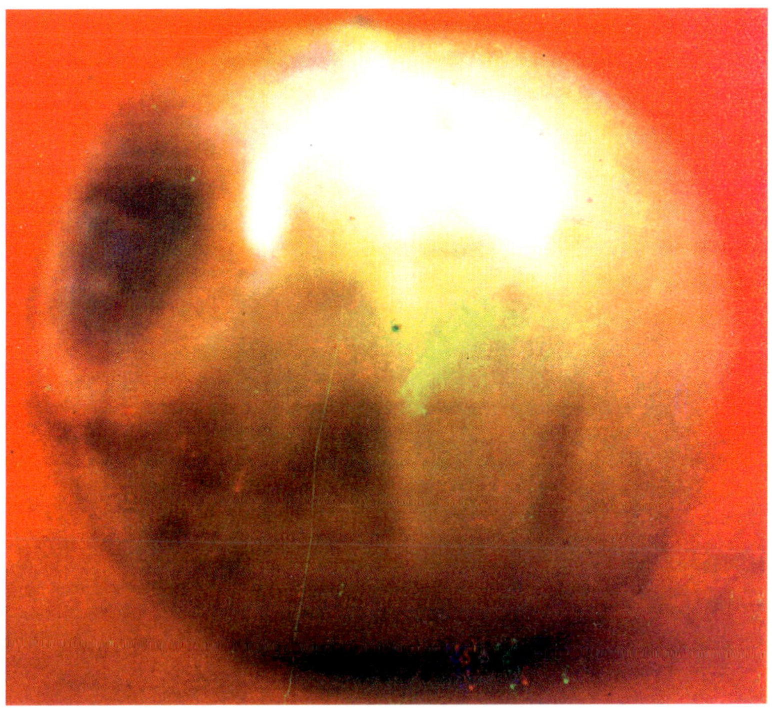

Rhizopus Rot of Amla

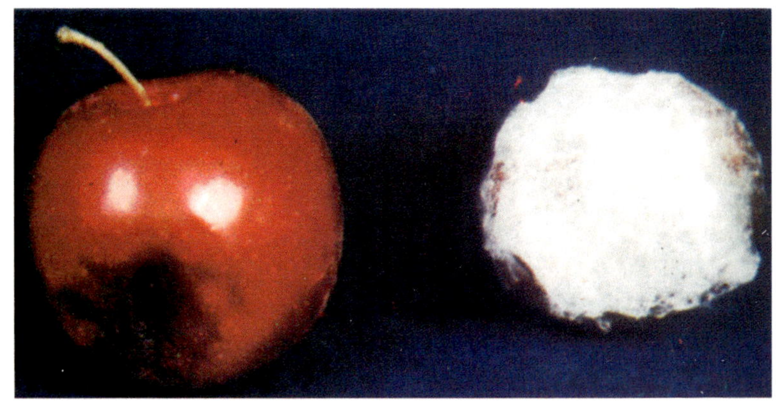

Rhizopus Rot of Plum

Aspergillus Rot of Plum

Aspergillus Rot of Pear

Penicillium Rot of Plum

**Aspergillus Rot of Lemon**

**Rot of Sweet Orange due to Aspergillus niger and Penicillium sp.**

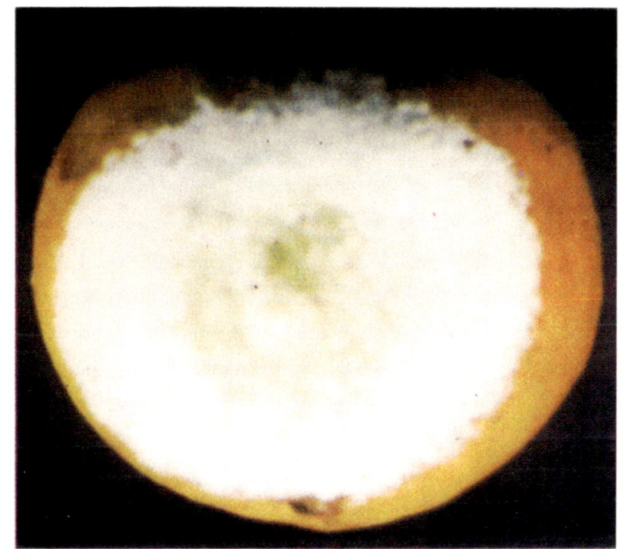

Penicillium Rot of Orange

Phytopthora Rot of Gauva

Aspergillus Rot of Pomegranate

**Control**

(a) Kapoor and Chohan (1974) reported that pre-harvest sprays of Ziram, Captan and Ferbam.

(b) Heat treatment has been used for sterilization and prevention of post-harvest diseases of papaya.

(c) Thiram, Ferbam and Captan completely inhibit the growth of M. phasceoli *in vitro*. Ziram and Captan provide best Protection and ferbam was found best in post-inoculation treatment. Thiram and Cuman inhibited the growth of the pathogens *in vitro* provides less efficient on fruits. Ziram is better *in vivo* than *in vitro* tests (Kapur and Chohan, 1974).

## 2. Post-harvest Rot of Papaya due to Botryodiploidia sp.

In Bihar, papaya is extensively grown in the districts of Ranchi and Bhagalpur. Prasad and Verma (1970) reported post-harvest rot of mature fruits due to Botryodiploidia theobromae pat. Tandon (1970) found rot of mummified fruits due to B. theobromae.

**Symptoms**

Water soaked lesions are formed on the infected fruits. In advanced cases, the affected region becomes dark brown and depressed. The spots are surrounded by water soaked areas which are grayish in colour. In the presence of high humidity and moderate temperature the water soaked spots get covered with light grey fungal growth. In severe cases, the pyenidia develop on affected patches of fruit. The mature fruits are more susceptible.

**Control**

1. Papaya fruits are highly perishable therefore proper handling of fruits during harvesting, packing and transportation helps to avoid injury to the fruits.
2. Removal and destruction of rotted fruits reduces sources of primary and secondary inoculum.
3. The hot water treatment combined with the vapor heat treatment provides adequate control of rot due to Botryodiplodia theobromae (Yaguchi and Nikamura, 1993).

### 3. Post-harvest rot of Papaya due to Rhizopus sp

Rhizopus is a very common fungus occur in godowns and storage houses of fruits. It grows only on fully mature injured fruits. Factors such as nature and type of wounds, rainfall, pre and post-harvest treatments and storage and transit conditions influence the development of Rhizopus rot of papaya (Nishijma, et al 1990).

#### Symptoms

The infected fruit of papaya possess irregular water soaked lesions, which gradually enlarge. The Rhizopus rot or watery fruit rot develops on the injured fruit. The lesions in due course are covered with whitish fungal growth. In advanced stages of rot development, the lesions turn dark brown due to sporulation of fungus. The heavily infected fruits become watery. Rhizopus rot emit dirty foul smell. Infection spread quickly to the adjourning fruits. The fruits finally collapse within 5-7 days of infection.

#### Cause

The watery rot of papaya is caused by Rhizopus stolonifer (Ehrex Fr.) Lind (Pathak, et. al.) (1990) and R. nigricans Ehrenb. Shrivastava, et al. (1964). The R. stolonifer attack only injured mature fruits.

#### Control

1. Post-harvest treatment of papaya with 100 ppm Aureofungin can control Rhizopus rot of papaya Sridhar (1974).
2. Dowicide at 2000 ppm also effective against Rhizopus rot.
3. Preharvest treatment of Captan 5000 ppm effective against watery rot of papaya (Pathak, et. al. 1976).
4. Field spray of Mancozeb reducing Rhizopus soft rot incidence by reducing field initiated fruit diseases (Nishijima, et. al. 1990).

### 4. Post-harvest Rot of Papaya due to Phomopsis sp.

#### Symptoms

Spots caused by Phomopsis are initially water soaked which later becomes sunken. In advance stages the lesion becomes dark brown to black in colour. The affected areas are surrounded by white raised tissue. The infected tissue becomes lucid and macerated.

**Cause**

Phomopsis caricae-papaya Petrak & Ciferri. The mycelium is septate, hyaline, in initial stages, later changes to pale yellow to yellowish brown in colour. The hyphae produce rod shaped conidiophores which are tapering towards the apex measuring 6.6-14.5 um in length, canidia are strait, non-septate. rod shaped, hyaline, 3.33-10.1 × 1.6-2.44 um in size. The fungus also produces pycnidia, are tough flask shaped, black with an opening at the anterior end measuring 132.6-321.5 um in diameter (Dhingra and Khare 1971).

**Control**

1. Pre harvest treatment of Benomyl, Captan and Mancozeb has been found effective in preventing symptoms of Phomopsis.

**5. Post-harvest Rot of Papaya due to Fusarium sp.**

The Fusarium is a very common soil borne saprophytic fungus in tropical areas.

**Symptoms**

Fusarium acuminatum causes rot of fruits before as well as after harvest of papaya fruit. The disease starts as a water soaked lesions which are more or less circular, depressed. The skin becomes watery and soft. The infected tissue losses its turgidity. High humidity is favourable for the advancement of Fusarial rot of papaya. White mycelial growth develops on the infected fruit.

F. equiseti is very common on fully ripen papaya fruit which causes water soaked lesions, that increase rapidly causing 100 per cent decay within 7-8 days. The fruit loose its shape and the tissue turns soft. Infected fruit get covered with white cottony mass of fungus. Artificial inoculation of F. oxysporium develops small circular lesion which increases gradually. In severe cases, an extensive growth of fungal mycelium occurs in the form of concentric rings. High humidity and temperature at 26°C is most favourable for development of rot. F. moniliformae causes water soaked lesions under moist conditions. Whole fruit get rotted within 6-8 days. Infected fruit emit fermented odour. Fruit get covered with white mycelial mass.

**Cause**

Fusarium moniliforme Shelodon (Arya, et al. 1986); F. equiseti (Corda) Sacc., F. oxysoporium Schlecht (Lal & Arya, 1982).

**Control**

1. Papaya is a soft fleshy fruit therefore, proper handling of fruits during harvesting, packing and storage helps in avoiding injuries to the fruit.
2. Infected fruits can reduce diseases intensity.

## 6. Post-harvest Rot of Papaya due to Colletotrichum sp.

Wangikar and Raut (1992) reported rot of papaya by Colletotrichum papaya. The infected fruit shows circular, slightly sunken spots of brown colour, 1-3 cm in diameter. Usually such spots become water soaked. In advance stages many spots mix to form a big patch. Under humid conditions, spores are formed on the infected fruit in the form of concentric rings.

Lal, et al. (1979) studied association of C. capsici with fruit rot of papaya. The harvested fleshy healthy ripe fruits of papaya inoculated with C. capsici shows water soaked circular lesions after 7-8 days of inoculation period. The circular spots were enveloped with brown mycelium. In severe cases, numerous acervuli are formed on infected areas of fruit. Dastur (1921) reported occurrence of C. capsici with papaya rots. Deighton (1936) reported rot of papaya to C. capsici.

## 7. Gloeosporium rots of Papaya

Grewal (1954) and Tandon (1967) described rot of papaya fruit due to the attack of Gloeosporium papayae P. Henn. Initially small water soaked spots appear on the fruits, that enlarge gradually to form circular dark brown lesion. The circular water soaked spots ooze watery juice that consists of fungal spores. Later on the centre of spot becomes sunken. In very advanced stage of disease development the spot get covered by black dot like fruiting bodies and spore mass.

**Cause**

Gloeosporium papayae P. Henn.

### Control

1. Spraying of Bordeaux mixture before harvest of fruits can control post-harvest rot.
2. Dipping the ripe fruit in 2000 ppm Bavistin can control rot of papaya.

## 8. Thielaviopsis Rot of Papaya

Ciferri (1927) reported soft rot of papaya by Thielaviopsis state of Ceratocystis paradoxa (Dade) and C. moreau. Tewari et. al. (1988) observed this rot in the market of Allahabad.

### Symptoms

The disease starts by forming watery spots on fruit surface which later get covered with black dark coloured fungal mycelium. Numerous spores are formed on spots. In severe cases, infected fruit lose its texture and shape. Rotted fruits emit dirty foul odour.

### Control

1. Tiwari, et al. (1988) found Bavistin and Tecto 40 most effective against rot disease.

# Post-harvest Diseases of Mango

Heavy loss of harvested fruits of mango caused due to fungal. bacterial and physiological aspects. There is much fungal form responsible for storage rot of mangoes which directly affect the economy of the country.

**Table 4.1: Post-harvest diseases of mango fruit**

| *Sr. No.* | *Fungus* | *Geography* | *References* |
|---|---|---|---|
| *1* | *2* | *3* | *4* |
| 01 | Colletotrichum gloeosporioides | Punjab, UP, Assam, Kerala, Bihar | McRao, (1924); Baker. (1938) |
| 02 | Diplodia natalensis | – | Sattar & Malik (1959) Chakravarti & Srivastava, (1964) |
| 03 | Aspergillus niger | – | Srivastava (1968) |
| 04 | Rhizopus arrhizaus | – | Thakur (1972) |
| 05 | Macrophomina magriferae | – | Tandon (1967) |
| 06 | Pestalotiopsis magniferae | – | Prakash & Srivastava (1987) |
| 07 | Phoma multirostrata | – | Mathur, et al. (1962) |
| 08 | Rhizopus oryzae | – | Thakur (1972) |
| 09 | R. stolonifer | – | Thakur (1972) |
| 10 | Phomopsis amraii | – | Tandon, et al, (1965) |
| 11 | P. magriferae | – | Laxminarayan and Reddy (1975) |

*(Table Contd...)*

| 1 | 2 | 3 | 4 |
|---|---|---|---|
| 12 | Botryodiploidia | – | Srivastava, et. al. (1965); Tandon (1967) |
| 13 | Bacillus subtilis | – | Patel & Padhye (1948) |
| 14 | Actinodochium jenkinsii | Ratnagiri & Vengurla | Uppal, et. al (1952) |
| 15 | Aspergillus nidulans | Lucknow | Das Gupta & Bhatt (1946) |
| 16 | Aspergillus variecolor | Lucknow Secandrabad (AP) | Mohanty (1948) |
| 17. | Cladosporium herbarum | Poona Common | Rao (1966); Chemma & Dani (1935) |
| 18 | Penicillium fellulanus | Saharanpur, UP | Sinha (1946) |
| 19 | Penicillium sp. | Poona | Rao (1966 b) |
| 20 | Phoma sp. | Poona | Kanitkar & Uppal (1939) |
| 21 | Phytopthora arecae | Common | Mc Rao (1924) |
| 22 | Sclerotium rolfsii | Delhi | Vir & Sharma (1965) |

## 1. Colletotrichum Rot of Mango

Fruit rot by Colletotrichum is a very common and widespread disease of mango. This is a very destructive disease in the storage and transit Rath and Mohanan (1986). Sohi (1975) reported 24 per cent decay of fruit from Bangalore market.

### Symptoms

The infected green fruit shows numerous oval or irregular, brown or dark brown lesions of variable sizes distributed over the fruit surface, which spoil the whole fruit. In advanced stages, the spots cover the whole area of fruit surface and degrade the quality of fruit. In moist weather, minute pustules are formed on affected area. The fully ripen infected fruit shows sunken, blackish brown blotches on which numerous hyphae and spores appear. The fruits which come in contact with diseased fruit get infected (Sohi, et al. 1973).

On severe infection surface cracks may appear on the fruits. Many of these spots mix to form bigger spots involving the whole fruit. The spots are often concentric at the stem-end region.

## Cause

Colletotrichum gloeosporioides var minor reported on mango by Simmonds (1965). The mycelium is septate, hyaline to darker, which produces abundant acervuli on fruit surface. Numerous conidiophores and conidia are formed. The conidia are hyaline non-septate and spherical to oblong with rounded ends. The temperature between 20-30°C and relative humidity 95-97 per cent is favourable for rot development.

## Control

1. The post-harvest rot of fruits can be controlled by dipping affected fruits in hot water at 51°C for 10-15 minutes before storage.
2. Tandon and Singh (1968) found dipping of fruits in hot water at 50-55°C temperature for 15 minutes effective against intensity of rot development.
3. Pre-harvest treatment of fruits with Blitox 50 or Fytolan 3 gm/liter of water or Bavistin 50 WP 2 gm/liter of water three times during the year can reduce post-harvest rot caused by Colletotrichum sp.
4. Sanitation is different method of reducing disease intensity in godowns.
5. Tandon and Singh (1968) reported exposure of fruits to hot air to reduce intensity of rot development.
6. *Gas treatment:* Treatment of fruits with ammonia, $SO_2$ and $CO_2$ gas restricts the growth of micro flora causing post-harvest rot of mango.
7. Sohi, et al. (1973) reported control of disease by dipping fruits in 5000 ppm Benomyl and 500 ppm Thiobendazole for few minutes.

## 2. Post-harvest Rot of Mango due to Aspergillus Niger

Aspergillus rot is very common in all parts of the country. It causes heavy loss of fruits. The disease is more serious during storage and marketing processes. It has been reported to cause losses from 25-35 per cent at Allahabad and Lucknow (Srivastava, 1968).

### Symptoms

Initially light brown circular patches appear at the stalk end region of fruit. Gradually a large circular spot is formed around the stalk end. In advanced stages, the stalk end region becomes sunken. The affected fruit becomes yellowish at the base. The skin of the fruit becomes soft and sunken. The circular spot around the stalk end region of fruit get covered with black conidial heads of pathogens within 5-6 days. The disease is also known as black rot disease. Minor injuries are responsible for black rot diseases of mango fruits. The fungus causes rot at any part of the fruit. The position of black mould lesion depends on the position of injury on the fruit. The optimum temperature for development of disease is 30°C.

### Cause

The black mould rot of mangos is caused by Aspergillus niger Van Tiegh (Srivastava, 1968). The causal agent produces extensive network of mycelial mat and numerous conidiophores at the affected areas on the rotted fruits. The conidiophores are smooth, septate, of variable length. It produces black conidial heads. Conidia are globose which are smooth or rough walled. The fungus also produces globose superficial sclerotia on older lesions. Pre-harvest association of Aspergillus spores with fruits causes post-harvest rot of fruits during storage periods.

### Control

1. Pathak and Sekhawat (1976) recommended hot water treatment (55°C for 5 minutes) could delay the fruit rot.
2. Post-harvest treatment with fungicides like Benomyl 1500 ppm suggested by Bhargava and Singh (1975).
3. Pandey, et al. (1980) suggested of Trifolin 100 ppm, Delan 1250 ppm as a post-harvest treatment to reduce black mould rot of mangoes.

4. Sorting, removal and destruction of affected fruits from storehouse reduces disease intensity to large extent.

## 3. Post-harvest Rot of Mango due to Rhizopus Sp.

The soft rot of fruits is a very important and common disease in storehouses of mango fruits. The fungus Rhizopus arrhizus causes post-harvest rot of mango. This rot causes 6.3 per cent loss of fruits reported by Thakur and Chenulu (1966).

### Symptoms

Infection starts with a light brown coloured circular lesion on the affected fruits. Gradually the circular lesions increase, simultaneously the fruit becomes yellowish and soft. In advanced stages of rot development, watery substance comes out from the centre of spot and patches get covered with fungal growth. Temperature between 20-40°C and 100 per cent humidity is highly favourable for the development of Rhizopus rot (Thakur, 1972).

### Cause

Rhizopus arrhizus causes soft rot of mango (Thakur and Chenulu, 1966): Thakur (1972) found two more species responsible for soft rot disease during storage of fruits i.e. R. oryzae and R. stolonifer. The mycelium of R. arrhizus shows poorly developed stolons, which do not form nodes regularly. The fungus, produces prostrate sporangiophores, rarely single and measuring 0.5-2 mm in length. All the branches produce sporangia which are spherical, 120-250 mm in diameter. Spores oval or round grayish brown measuring 4.8–7.0 × 4.8–5.6 mm. and easily discriminated by wind.

### Control

1. Arrival of post-harvest rot can be prevented for about 20 days by dipping mango fruits in 2-aminothiazole with 2-aimnopyridine (each in 5% concentration) suggested by Thakur and Chenulu (1970).
2. Sanitation prevents rot of another fruits from soft rot symptoms.
3. Avoid injury to the fruit.

4. Pathak, et al. (1971) suggested method of prevention by using combination of oils like mustard oil, castor oil, liquid paraffin and per cent soap solutions.

## 4. Post-harvest Rot of Ripe Mango due to Diplodia sp.

The disease is known as stem end rot of mango. It occurs very commonly in godowns of ripe mango. The Diploidia rot of mango firstly reported by Chakravarti and Srivastava (1964) and also reported 4-6 per cent loss of fruits every year in India.

### Cause

The stem end rots of ripe mango caused by Diplodia natalensis P. Evans. The disease is characterised by discoloration of the stem ends of the mature fruits that leads to gradual darkening and withering. Later on the dark areas get covered with hyphal and conidial mass of fungus. The conidiophores of Diploidia are slender with dark bicelled, ellipsoidal conidia. It also produces globose, ostiolate, immersed pycnidia in advanced stages of rot disease.

Humid conditions are highly favourable for rot development. The affected fruit becomes dark black within 3-4 days. The pulp of affected fruits loose turgidity beccmes soft and turns brownish.

### Control

1. Injuries should be avoided during harvest.
2. Fruits can also be given post-harvest dip with Borax at 43°C temperature for three minutes.
3. Removal and destruction of infected fruits can reduce stem and rot for large extent.

## 5. Pestalotia Rots of Mango

The fruits get infected before harvest. The pathogen remains associated with affected green and immature fruits, which later cause post-harvest rot of ripe mango in storehouses. There are many species of Pestalotia responsible for rot diseases of mango are Pestalotia mangiferae (Baksh and Srivastava, 1987); P. dichaeta (Viegàs, 1946); P. funerea (Wardhaw and Leonard, 1936); P. versicolor (Anonymous, 1974-85) and P. glandicola (Ullasa and Rawel, 1975).

### Symptoms

A dark brown, circular lesion occurs all over the fruit. In severe cases the spots increases and becomes dark black in colour. The lesions ooze sticky, yellowish fluid from the centre of the spot. The lesions get covered with blackish hyphal growth and pustules. The optimum temperature for development of rot is in between 20-25°C.

### Control

1. The extract of Lycopodium clavatum can control post-harvest rot by Diploidia sp. (Khanna and Chandra, 1978).

## 6. Post-harvest Rot of Mango due to Phoma sp.

Phoma multirostrata causes rot of mango fruit (Prakash and Singh, 1976; Prakash and Raoof, 1985; Arya and Mathew, 1991). The affected fruits show sunken brown coloured spots which increase gradually by the age of fruit. In severe cases numerous small black pycnidia are formed on the infected region of the fruit. Pre-harvest spray treatment of fruits can control Phoma rot of mango. Arya and Mathew (1991) tried three systemic fungicides i.e. Bavistin, Delan and Derosol for control of the disease. Derosol found most effective against phoma rot.

## 7. Botryodiploidia Rots of Mango

The fungus is aggressive, vigorous and universal in distribution. This disease is most serious during storage and marketing of fruits. The fungus remains associated with fruit before harvest, latter it causes post-harvest rots during transportation and storage of fruits. The disease is also known as soft rot of mango.

### Symptoms

The infection usually starts at the injured site of fruit or at the stalk end region of the fruit. It causes water soaked lesions and in severe cases whole fruit get infected. The central part of infected area becomes dark brown in colour which is surrounded by peripheral zone of light brown colour. The margin of large patches is generally irregular in outline and appear water soaked. Many black dots like pycnidia develop in later stages of rot development. The moderate temperature 25°C and high humidity favours the rot development.

## Cause

Soft rot of mango is caused by Botryodiploidia theobromae pat. (Srivastava. et al. 1965.; Tandon, 1967).

## Control

1. Spalding & Reeder (1986) recommended hot water treatment of fruits at 53° C temperatures for 3 minutes. Imazalil (0.1%) treatment & gamma radiation (0.2 k gm) for the control of Botryodiploidia rot of mango during storage.

## 8. Storage Rots of Mango due to Macrophomina

Chaube (1984) reported storage rot of mango by Macrophomina mangiferae Hingorani, et al. (1960). The affected fruits shows water soaked round lesions which enlarge gradually and cause rot in the storage. Removal and destruction of affected fruits can reduce disease intensity.

# Post-harvest Diseases of Apple *(Pyrus malus)*

An apple is one of the most popular fruits in the world. It is commonly grown in the Northern temperature zone in both hemisphere. It belongs to the rose family Rosaceae. Its Botanical name is Pyrus malus. The fruits covered by thin glossy skin. As the fruit ripens, the starch it contains becomes changed into sugar. The fruits are harvested still they are hard and having reached the proper development.

An apple has better storage capability then most other fruits. Cost-wise, apples are expensive. During storage and transit, it is attacked by fungal species. The post-harvest disease of apple is as follow:

**Table 5.1: Post-harvest rot of apple**

| *Sl. No.* | *Fungus* | *Geographical area* | *Reference* |
|---|---|---|---|
| *1* | *2* | *3* | *4* |
| 01 | Gilberella persicaria | Allahabad (U.P.) | Mehrotra and Mehrotra (1963) |
| 02 | Gliocephalotrichum bulbilium | Allahabad (U.P.) | Khanna and Chandra (1975 b) |
| 03 | Memnoniella ehinata | Poona, Maharashtra | Rao (1966 b). |
| 04 | Mucor mucedo | Bombay, Maharashtra | Rao (1966 b) |
| 05 | Paecilomyces variotii | Allahabad | Tandon, et al. (1975) |

*(Table Contd...)*

| 1 | 2 | 3 | 4 |
|---|---|---|---|
| 06 | P. expansum<br>P. purpurogenum | Lucknow,<br>Chaubattia<br>UP | Sing (1943 b)<br>Sinha (1946)<br>Tandon, et al. (1975) |
| 07 | Phytopthora cactorum | Chaubattia, UP | Singh (1946 b) |
| 08 | Penicillium funiculosum | - | Brown and Hendrix (1978) |
| 09 | Pezicula malicortics | - | Brown and Hendrix (1978) |
| 10 | Phoma sp. | - | Brown and Hendrix (1978) |
| 11 | Pleospora herbarum | - | Raina, et al. (1971) |
| 12 | Trichothecium roseum | - | Raina, et al. (1971) |
| 13 | Colletotrichum gloeosporioides | | Tandon and Verma (1963) |
| 14 | Glomerella cingulata | - | Chand, et al. (1968) |

## 1. Post-harvest Rot of Apple due to Alternaria sp.

The possibilities of rotting of apple fruit increases if the apples are still on the tree or stored for several months in godowns. Combrink, et al. (1985) isolated and identified Alternaria alternata from the rotted part of the apple. The Alternaria alternata can be identified due to presence of muriform canidia arranged in chains. The conidiophores are single or branched arising singly or in group, straight or flexuous, smooth or rough. The canidia are with eight transverse and several longitudinal septa. The conidia are obclavate, ovoid or ellipsoid with short beak and are arranged in a chain. In storehouses, the fungus grows on the apple fruit and penetrates inside the pulp. The Alternaria rot of fruits develop slowly. The symptoms appear after a few months.

### Symptoms

The disease appears in the form of brown spots on the stem end region of apple or anywhere on the fruit surface. Gradually the spots become dark brown to black in colour. The spot shows concentric rings. The pulp of fruit below the spot turn brown that emit fermented odour.

### Cause

Alternaria alternate (Fr.) Keissler.

### Control

1. Fruit contamination with Alternaria spores can be reduced by dipping fruits in Chlorinated water before storage.
2. Careful handling and sorting of fruits during harvest and packing can reduce disease intensity during storage.

## 2. Post-harvest Rot of Apple due to Botryotinia_sp.

The Botryotinia rot of apple is of major importance because it causes heavy loss of apple because of fast spreading tendency of pathogen.

### Symptoms

The fungus produces different types of symptoms on fruits. Slight red coloured spots formed on the fruit. The spots turn dark brown coloured. In severe cases the fruit pulp gets converted into soft brown rot. The injured fruits get infected easily. Humid conditions and low temperature are highly favourable for grey mould rot of apple.

Heavily affected fruit get covered with grey moldy growth of fungus. It also produces black tough sclerotia of few millimeters in size.

### Cause

Grey mould rot of apple caused by Botryotinia fuckeliana (de Bary) Whetzel.

### Control

1. Tronsmo and Yastaas (1980) controlled the disease by spraying the blossom with antagonistic fungus Trichoderma viride that reduces post-harvest rot of fruits.
2. Beattie and Outhred (1970) suggested dipping of the fruits in hot water immediately after harvest.

## 3. Post-harvest Rots of Apple due to Colletotrichum sp.

Colletotrichum rot of apple was firstly reported in India by Chand, et al. (1968).

**Symptoms**

The infected fruit shows light brown coloured spots. Later on the spot becomes rough, circular and depressed. In advanced stages of rot, dark black, dot like acervuli are formed on the affected areas. The skin ruptures and spore mass of dark brown colour exposed out. The disease is also common in apple orchards as well as in storage. The optimum temperature for development of rot is 20°C.

**Cause**

The causal agent is Colletotrichum gloeosporioides (Penz). The mycelium is grey with orange coloured spore masses. The conidia are uni-nucleate with rounded ends that vary in size and shape.

**Control**

1. Remove infected mummified fruits from orchard as well as from storehouses to reduce diseases intensity.
2. Spray trees with fungicides several times during growing time to control pre- and post-harvest rots.

### 4. Post-harvest Rots of Apple due to Rhizopus sp.

It is a very important post-harvest disease of apple. It causes heavy loss of fruits during transportation and storage. It is also known as Whisker's rot disease.

**Symptoms**

Brown patches are formed on fruits. The Skin becomes loose that can be easily peeped from the underlying tissue. The brown spots get converted into water soaked spots during advancement of the rot disease. The affected tissue becomes soft. The infected fruit oozes watery juicy substance of acidic odour. In severe cases, complete fruit get covered with loosely arranged fungal hyphae and black fruiting bodies. Optimum temperature for rot development is 36°C (Bhargava and Gupta, 1957).

**Cause**

The post-harvest rot of apple caused due to Rhizopus arrhizus A. Fischer. It is easily identified due to its coarse white mouldy strands of hyphae and globular white spore heads, which later turn black.

**Control**

1. During storage, the fruits should be dipped into fungicide solution of Carbendazim (1gm/liter water) for 5 minutes.
2. Care should be taken during harvest to avoid injury.
3. Storage of fruits at 4-50°C temperature can restrict the Rhizopus rot.
4. The fruits should be treated with post-harvest fungicides (Thakur and Chemulu, 1970).

## 6. Blue Mould Rot of Apple

The post-harvest rot is also known as soft rot or wet rot disease. Several species of Penicillium cause blue mould rot of apple. The disease initiate on any part of the fruit. Improper ventilation amounting to high temperature during transportation and storage aggravate the blue mold rot.

**Symptoms**

Light brown discoloured spots appear on affected fruits which later become soft and watery in texture. The discoloured spots become circular and get covered with white growth of fungus, which later produces blue green spores. A characteristic moldy odour is emitted from the infected fruits. The rotted areas do not become sunken.

**Cause**

The blue mould disease is caused by Penicillium expansum Thom. The mycelium is septate, huge with numerous blue green canidia in the form of chains.

**Contro**

1. Affected fruits must be collected and destroyed.
2. Handle fruits carefully during harvest, packing and transit to avoid injury to the fruits.
3. Washing of fruits with clean and hydro cooling can avoid post-harvest rot caused due to Penicillium.
4. Smith and Anderson (1975) suggested controlled atmospheric storage of apple fruits to avoid blue mould disease.

5. Gerhardt (1942) recommended treatment of $CO_2$ gas to the fruits to avoid blue mould rot during transit.

6. Thiobendazole and Sodium Orthophenylphenate (SOPP 0.2%) have also been used for control for post-harvest rot or blue mould disease of apple.

## 7. Phytopthora Rots of Apple

It is also one of the important rot disease occur in orchards as well as in storage. It is very common in apple growing areas. The fruits get affected before harvest. The fallen fruits severe as a source of inoculum. The fungus causes post-harvest rot of apple during storage.

### Symptoms

The affected fruits posses light brown discoloured spots. In severe cases the flesh of the fruit becomes brownish and watery. The hyaline hyphal threads are seen under the skin of infected fruits as well as on the surface of infected fruits. The affected fruits also retain firm texture.

### Cause

Collar rot of apple caused by Phytopthora cactorum (Lebert and Cohn). The mycelium is hyaline, coenocytic, produces sporangia which measure 4-6 nm. High humidity and low temperature (18-22°C) is highly favourable for development of Phytopthera sp. The sporangia germinate directly by forming germ tube.

### Control

1. The fruit should be sprayed by systemic fungicide before harvest.

2. Do not keep fruits on soil surface during harvest.

3. Discard infected fruits from storehouses.

4. Clean and dry weather of godown can control Phytopthora rot.

# 6

# Post-harvest Diseases of Pineapple (Ananas cosmos) L. Mer.

The pineapple fruits are sword-shaped surrounded by crown of stiff leaves. After fruiting, if the fruit is removed, another fruiting stem arising at the same place. This process being repeated usually for 10 years. It is extensive in tropical and subtropical fields.

**Table 6.1: Post-harvest rots of pineapple**

| *Sr. No.* | *Fungus* | *Geography* | *Reference* |
|---|---|---|---|
| 01 | Botryodiplodia ananassae | Allahabad (UP) | Tandon & Bhargave (1962) |
| 02 | Fusarium solani | Bombay (MS) Jabalpur (MP) | Rao (1966b) Sharma, et al. (1981) |
| 03 | Ceratocystis paradoxa | Poona (MS) Bangalore (Karnataka) | Mehta, (1940) |

## 1. Post-harvest Rot of Pineapple due to Ceratocystis sp.

The disease is also known as soft rot or core rot or black rot disease of pineapple. It is firstly reported by Mehta in 1940. Later on it is studied by Rao (1966 b) and Shridhar (1975). It is a destructive disease commonly occurs in godowns and during transportation of fruits.

### Symptoms

The infected fruits show water soaked lesions which turn yellowish and in severe cases becomes dark black. Lateran many spots coal sac to form a large patch. The tissue under the black patches becomes black, soft and watery. In severe case of infection the entire fruit may turn dark and rot. It oozes watery substance upon little pressure. The rotted fruits emit dirty foul odour.

### Cause

The black rot of pineapple is caused by Ceratocystis paradoxa (Dade) Moreau (Mehta, 1940). It is a saprophytic fungus. It can grow on wide range of hosts. It enters the fruits through injured passages of the fruit.

### Control

1. Disease free suckers should be planted to avoid post-harvest rot of pineapple.
2. Collect and discard diseased fruits from storehouses.
3. The injured spaces of fruits should be treated with 10 per cent solution of benzoic acid in alcohol.
4. Spraying of 0.1 per cent benzoic acid in kaoline reduces this disease during transportation (Mallikaryunaradhya, et al. 1979).
5. During packing of fruits, the containers should be sprayed with 3 per cent formalin.
6. Dry the fruits in sunlight for 2 hours.
7. Do not keep harvested fruits on soil surface during packing.
8. Sridhar (1975) suggested post-harvest dipping of fruits for 5 minutes in Thiobendazole 1000 ppm.

## 2. Botryodiploidia Rot of Pineapple

Fruit rot of pineapple caused by few of the saprophytic fungi, which are capable of infecting fruits during transit and storage. The Botryodiploidia rot have been reported by Tandon and Bhargava (1962) from the market of Allahabad. The disease is most severe during transportation.

### Symptoms

Only the injured fruits are highly susceptible for the Botryadiplodia rot. Initially, the skin of fruit near injured area becomes yellowish followed by appearance of water soaked lesions. Infection start from the water soaked spots and gradually rotting progresses to the remaining part of the fruit. The infected tissue of fruit looses its turgidity and becomes watery and turns dark brown in colour. In severe cases white or light grey cottony growth of fungus appear on the rotted tissues, which later get covered with Pycnidia. The mature ripen fruits are more susceptible for the poor-harvest rot.

**Cause**

The disease is caused by Botryodiplodia ananassae (Sacc.) Peter. Tandon and Bhargava (1962). The fungus produces flask shaped Pycnidia having neck and osliole. The fruiting bodies occur in groups. The fungus also produces short conidiophores and bicelled, brown coloured comida at its tip. The temperature between 26-30°C is highly favourable for storage rot disease of pineapple by the growth of Botryodiploidia sp.

**Control**

1. The fruits should be free from any injury during storage.
2. Ripening of fruits during transportation should be avoided.
3. Collect and discard affected fruits from godowns.
4. Care should be taken during picking of fruits to avoid fruit injury.
5. Clean and aerated godowns can help to avoid Botryodiplodia rot of pineapple.

# Post-harvest Rots of Pomegranate

**Table 7.1: Post-harvest rots of pomegranate**

| *Sr. No.* | *Fungus* | *Geography* | *Reference* |
|---|---|---|---|
| *1* | *2* | *3* | *4* |
| 01 | Aspergillus avamori | Lucknow | Anonymous (1950) |
| 02 | A. castaneus | Allahabad (UP) | Butler , (1914b) |
| 03 | A. clavatum | Meerut (UP) | Sinha (1946) |
| 04 | A. flavus | Hissar | Shrivastava, et al. (1964) |
| 05 | A. foetidus | Haryana | Shrivastava & Tandon (1971) |
| 06 | A. funmigatus | Cuttack | Shrivastava, et al. (1964) |
| 07 | A. nidulaus | Orissa | Vyas, (1976) |
| 08 | A. niger | Jabalpur (MP) | Ratnam and Neema (1967) |
| 09 | Cephalosporium acremonium | Hissar (Haryana) | – |
| 10 | Cladosporium orysporium | Jodhpur Rajasthan | Panwar and Vyas (1974) |
| 11 | Curvularia Pallescens | Lucknow (UP) | Shrivastava, et al (1964). Vyas (1976) |
| 12 | Glomerella cingulata | Ludhiana (Punjab) | Singh & Chovan, (1972a) |

*(Table Contd...)*

| 1 | 2 | 3 | 4 |
|---|---|---|---|
| 13 | Paecilomyces | Lucknow (UP) | Shrivastava, et al. (1964) |
| 14 | Penicillium atramentosum | Lucknow (UP) | Sinha (1946) |
| 15 | Penicillium | Meerut (UP) | Shrivastava, et al. (1964) |
| 16 | Rhizopus arrhizus | Hissar (Haryana) | Chandra & Tandon (1965c) |
| 17 | R. stolonifer | Hissar (Haryana) | – |
| 18 | Sclerotium rolfsi | Hissar (Haryana) | Uppal, et al. (1933), Kanwar & Thakur (1973) |
| 19 | S. rolfsii | | Shrivastava, et al. (1964) |
| 20 | Phomopsis sp. | – | – |

## 1. Aspergillus Rots of Pomegranate

Srivastava, et al. (1964) reported post-harvest rot of pomegranate due to Aspergillus flavus. Aspergillus rot usually starts ás water soaked spots with brownish colour. The lesions enlarge with the age of fruit. The enlarged spots get depressed at the centre. In severe cases dull greenish mouldy growth of A. flavus appears on the infected surface of the fruit. This is a common destructive fungus cause's heavy loss of fruits during transit and storage. The injured fruits are highly susceptible for the attack of rot causing fungi. A. flavus also causes post-harvest of different types of fruits. A. flavus rot of Ber (Mitter and Tandon, 1930); A. flavus rot of papaya (Srivastava, et. al. (1964); A. flavus rot of Banana (Srivastava, et. al. 1964); A. flavus rot of guava (Lal, et al. (1980), A. avamori causes rot of pomegranate (Anonymous, 1950); A. castaneus rot of Pomegranate (Butler, 1914 b); A. Clavatum rot of Pomegranate (Sinha, 1946); A. foetidus rot of pomegranate (Srivastava, et al, 1964); A fumigatus rot of Pomegranate by Srivastava, et al, 1964); A. nidulance rot of Pomegranate (Vyas, 1976); A. niger rot of Pomegranate (Ratnam and Neema, 1967).

### Control

Pre-storage treatment of fruits with Benlate (2000 ppm) effective the aspergillus rots.

### 2. Penicillium Rot of Pomegranate

Srivastava, et al (1964) explained the post-harvest rot of pomegranate caused by Penicillium expansum. There are many species of Penicillium responsible for post-harvest rot of perishables during transit and storage. P. atramentosum causes post-harvest rot of pomegranate during storage (Sinha, 1946); The P. expansum causes severe deterioration of pomegranate. The injured and mature fruits get infected easily, because the fungus scurvies on dead plant material and the spores are of common occurrence in the atmosphere. Rot of injured fruits start after the attack of fungus, P. expansum produces light brown coloured spots on fruits, in initial stages. The infected area become mushy and can be easily identified from healthy tissue. The infected areas become soft, pale brown, which get covered with white mouldy growth of fungus. In severe cases, the affected areas get covered with numerous greys to blue coloured spores. Development of disease accelerated due to high humidity and high temperature. P. expansum also causes blue mould rot of apple (Brain, et al. 1956; Wilson and Nuovo, 1973); Rot of grapes caused due to P. citrinum (Tandon, et al. 1975); Grape rot by P. chrysogenum (Singh and Kainsa, 1983); P. Crustosum causes rot of Ber (Badyal and Sumbali, 1990); Papaya rot by P. implicatum (Dhingra and Khare, 1971); P. frequentans responsible for rot of fruits of pear, plum and peach. P. funiculosum causes apple rot during storage (Brown and Hendrix, 1978). Citrus fruit rot cause by P. crustosum (Garcha and Singh, 1976) P. digitatum (Butler & Bishy, 1931; Roy, 1948; Thom, 1930). P. fellutanum (Sinha, 1946) and P. italicum (Roy, 1949). There are reports of fruit rot of Zizyphus sp. caused by Penicillium sp. (Saha, 1945). Penicillium rots of Indian gooseberry reported by Shrivastava, et al. (1964).

### 3. Post-harvest Rot due to Rhizopus sp.

Chandra and Tandon (1965 c) reported Rhizopus arrhizus is the cause of decay of Pomegranate fruits from Hissar (Haryana) market. The disease is characterised by the production of irregular water soaked lesions which are light brown in colour. The intensity of disease depends on the maturity and variety of fruits. The spots grow in regular manner and subsequently get covered by fungal growth which remains white when young but turn dark brown with age. The disease is characterised by rapid tissue disintegration. The fruits turn soft and finally collapse. In severe cases, watery substance comes out from the infected fruits.

### Cause

Rhizopus arrhizus Fischer (Chandra & Tandon, 1965c). Different Rhizopus species are responsible for post-harvest rot of different types of fruits. Post-harvest rot of Banana by R. oryzae (Anonymous, 1962 a); Storage rot of Citrus by R. nigricans (Ratnam and Nema, 1967; Sinha, 1946); Fruit rot of Guava by R. nigricans (Shrivastava and Tandon, 1964); post-harvest rot of Jack fruit by R. artocarpi (Tilak & Rao, 1970); fruit rot of litchi by Rhizopus sp. (Sharma and Tewari, 1969); storage of papaya by R. arrhizus & nigricans (Goal, et al. 1971) and Shrivastava and Tandon (1964).

### Control

1. Post-harvest treatment with 100 ppm Aureofungin restricts the rot development.
2. Washing of fruits with 2000 ppm Dowicide or 2000 ppm Captan checks the rot caused by Rhizopus.

### 4. Post-harvest Rot due to Sclerotium sp.

Post-harvest rot of pomegranate fruits during transit and storage due to presence of Sclerotium roilfsi reported by Uppal, et al. (1935); Kanwar & Thakur (1973) in Haryana. The infection starts on any place on the fruit, especially at the site of injury. The infected area becomes water soaked and soft. In advanced stages that turn brownish to dark brown in colour. In severe cases of rot development, whitish, fluddy mycelial growth appears on the affected area. The S. rolfsii has wide variety of host range. It is also responsible for the post-harvest rot of different types of fruits. Apple rot (Sumbhali and Mehrotra, 1980); Sclerotial rot of Banana (Uppal, et. al. 1935); Sclerotial rot of Mango fruit (Vir and Sharma, 1965); Papaya rot (Uppal, et. al. 1935); Zizyphus rot (Misra and Khare, 1970) occur during transportation and storage of fruits.

### Cause

Sclerotium rolfsi Sacc.

### Control

1. Avoid keeping fruits on soil surface during harvest.
2. Fruit wash with Diathane Z-78 (1000 ppm) before storage controls white rot development during storage

## 5. Post-harvest Rot due to Cladosporium Oxysporium

Panvar and Vyas (1974) reported Cladosporium rot of pomegranate from Jodhpur (Rajasthan) market. The disease starts as discoloured spots on the skin of mature fruits. In advanced stages, light blue to greenish coloured spots are formed The disease progresses in a circular manner. Light yellow to brown coloured mycelian growth of the fungus occurs on the affected areas. The row shows dark brown coloured large necrotic lesion, which makes fruits unfit for utilisation. The same pathogen also cause post-harvest rot of fruits of chilli (Panvar and Vyas, 1974); and rot of zyzipus fruit (Panvar and Vyas, 1974); Fruit rot of Banana (Uppal, et al, 1935); Fruit rot of grapes (Wangikar, et al, 1969 b).

### Cause

Cladosporium oxysporium Berk. & Curt.

### Control

1. Hot water treatment for 5 minutes at 40° C temperature checks the rot development.
2. The clean and aerated godown can prevent losses of fruits caused due to Cladosporium species.

# Post-harvest Diseases of Amla (Emlica Afficinalis)

The fruit of amla is one of the richest sources of Vit-C. It consists of 500 to 780°mg of Vit-C per 100 grams of edible part. Vit-C is very important antioxidant that plays an important role in human body which erace free radicals and prevents the body from different types of diseases.

**Table 8.1: Post-harvest rot of amla**

| *Sr. No.* | *Fungi* | *Geography* | *Reference* |
|---|---|---|---|
| *1* | *2* | *3* | *4* |
| 01 | Aspergillus niger | Allahabad (UP) | Shrivastava, et al. (1964) Shrivastava & Tandon (1968) |
| 02 | Cladosporium cladosporioides | Allahabad (UP) | Jamaluddin (1978) |
| 03 | Cladosporium herbarium | Allahabad (UP) | Tandon & Verma (1978) |
| 04 | Penicillium islandicum | Varanasi (UP) | Setty (1959) |
| 05 | Phoma putaminum | Allahabad (UP) | Pandey, et al. (1980) Shrivastava, et al. (1968) |
| 06 | Cladosporium tenuissimum | – | Jalaluddin, (1978) |

*(Table Contd...)*

| 1 | 2 | 3 | 4 |
|---|---|---|---|
| 07 | Phomopsis phyllanthi | Allahabad (UP) | Lal, et. al. (1982) |
| 08 | Penicillium sp. | – | Srivastava et. al. (1964 b) |
| 09 | Pestalotia cruenta | Allahabad (UP) | Shrivastava, et al. (1964 b) |
| 10 | Cladosporium tenuissium | Allahabad (UP) | Jamaluddin, (1978) |

## 1. Post-harvest Rot of Amla due to Aspergillus Niger

Aspergillus niger survives in soil and decaying plant material as a saprophyte. Shrivastava, et al. (1964). Shrivastava and Tandon (1968) reported post-harvest rot of amla due to Aspergillus niger. This fungus enters the fruit thróugh stalk end injury or from any injured space on the fruit. The infected fruits shows circular lesion with distinct discoloured margin. The lesion increases in regular manner. In case of heavy infection, the infected areas of the fruit get enveloped with black mouldy growth of fungus. The whole fruit get deteriorated within 8-10 days of infection.

### Cause

Aspergillus niger van Tiegh.

A. niger also causes typical stalk rot symptoms in grapes (Singh and Kainsa, 1983). Black mould rot of mango (Das Gupta and Bhatt, 1946; Shrivastava, et al., 1965; Srivastava, 1966).

### Control

1. Bhargava and Singh, (1975) recommended post-harvested dip treatment with fungicide like banomyl 1500 ppm in case of mango rot. It is also effective against black mould rot of Amla.
2. Post-harvest fruit dip in hot water can reduce disease incidence.
3. Careful handling is necessary at all the stages during harvest and after harvest especially during transit and storage.

4. Aerated storehouse also reduces disease intensity.
5. The fruits should be free from infection before packing and transportation.
6. Heating up of stored fruits should also be avoided.

## 2. Post-harvest Rot of Amla due to Penicillium sp.

The Penicillium rot of Amla is described by Setty (1959) and Shrivastava et al. (1964) from the market of Allahabad (U.P.). The infection was severe among injured fruits of amla. The fungus cause fruit decay during storage. The infection starts from an injury to the fruit. The infected fruits get covered with fungal growth which is slightly raised. Within 4-5 days of infection, the infected area shows heavy sporulation of dull green colour. Such fruits are unfit for consumption.

### Cause

The causal organism of fruit rot amla is Penicillium islandicum Sopp.

The rot occurs more often on fallen fruits. The susceptibility of fruits towards blue mould not of amla increases when fruits kept for storage and marketing.

### Control

1. The clean and aerated godowns can prevent Penicillium rot of fruits.
2. Five minutes dip of fruits in 2 per cent bleaching powder and 10 minutes dip in 0.2 per cent bleaching powder checks the Penicillium rot of amla.

## 3. Post-harvest Rot of Amla due to Cladosporium sp.

The post-harvest rot of Amla is caused by Cladosporium herbarum (Tandon and Varma, 1964) and C. cladosporioide (Jamaluddin, 1978). The rot caused by C. tennissimum (Jamaluddin, 1978) commences as small circular spots on fruit surface. The light brown mycelium grown on the infected area. The affected area does not spread very fast. The rot caused by C. cladosporioides shows dark brown necrotic spot on the infected fruits. All the species of Cladosporium causes dry rot of amla.

## Cause

Cladosporium cladosprioides (Fries) de Vries.

**Control:** 1. Hot water treatment of fruits at 52° C temperatures for 5 minutes can prevent Cladosporium rot of amla.

# 9

# Post-harvest Disease of Citrus Fruits

## LEMONS

Citrus fruits are cultivated throughout the world, primarily in subtropical areas. Citrus fruits are eaten fresh.

Lemons are acidic fruits borne on a small tree. Fruits are sour, oblong to avoid, soft walled. Because of its profuse fruiting of the lemon tree is pruned more extensively. Fully, mature fruits are picked for size, generally white still green and held in storage, until properly cured. If properly picked and stored, they can be held for several months after picking. In storage the skin of the green lemon turns to a wary yellow. The injured fruits get attacked by during storage; even uninjured fruits get lost due to unhealthy storage facilities. The post-harvest rots of lemon listed below.

## ORANGE

The production of oranges ranks first among tree fruits produced in the Western Hemisphere. The cultivated oranges consist chiefly of three main types.

1. The sour orange (C. aurantiuw).
2. The mandarin oranges of which many types exist. (C. nobilis). These are mostly loose skinned types which are not so extensively grown as the sweet oranges but are highly popular because of their flavour.
3. The sweet orange (O. sinensis) which has many varieties.

Oranges are picked by hand labour and ladders are placed around the outside of the tree from which all of the fruit is reached. The fruit is immediately halted from the grove where it enters either the packing plant for preparation of transport. The oranges are degreased by placing in storage rooms.

**Table 9.1: Post-harvest rots of citrus fruits**

| *Sr. No.* | *Fungus* | *Geography* | *Reference* |
|---|---|---|---|
| *1* | *2* | *3* | *4* |
| 01 | Alternaria citri | Ajmer Rajasthan Jabalpur Poona (M.H.) Kalimpong (WB) Punjab | Jyoti & Vashist (1959): Agrawal & Hasija (1961c); Agarwal & Hasiya (1967); Roy (1941): Uppal, et al. (1935) |
| 02 | Aspergillus aculeatus | Faizabad (UP) | Cash & Watson (1935) |
| 03 | A. niger | Allahabad (UP) Kalimpong (WB) Jabalpur (MP) | Shrivastava & Tandon (1969b); Roy (1948); Ratnam & Nema. (1967) |
| 04 | Botryodiploidia theobromae | Allahabad (UP) Jabalpur (MP) | Shrivastava, et al. (1964); Roy, (1965b) |
| 05 | Candida krusei | Nagpur | Shankarpal (1976) |
| 06 | Ceratocystis fimbriata | Varanasi (UP) | Singh and Basu (1974) |
| 07 | Cladosporium herbarum | Allahabad (UP) | Tandon & Verma (1964) |
| 08 | C. sphaerospermum | Delhi | Gaur & Chenulu (1981) |
| 09 | Colletotrichum gloeosporioides | Amritsar (Punjab) Lucknow (UP) | Uppal, et al. (1935); Thind & Rawla (1961b) |
| 10 | Diplodia natalensis | Poona, Nagpur | Patel, et al. (1949), Shinde & Asalmol, (1968-69) |
| 11 | Fusarium solani | Udaipur (Rajasthan) Allahabad (UP) | Bhatnagar & Prasad, (1966b) Jamaluddin (1974) |
| 12 | Oospora citriaurantii | Common | Butler & Bisby, (1931) |

*(Table Contd...)*

| 1 | 2 | 3 | 4 |
|---|---|---|---|
| 13 | Penicillium crustosum | Ludhiana (Punjab) | Garcha & Singh (1976) |
| 14 | P. digitatum | Kalimpong (WB)<br>Delhi | Butler & Bisby (1931),<br>Roy (1948)<br>Thom (1030) |
| 15 | P. expansum | Kalimpong (WB)<br>Bornihat<br>(Assam) | Roy (1949)<br>Bhattacharya and<br>Baruah (1953) |
| 16 | P. fellutanum | Allahabad (UP) | Sinha (1946) |
| 17 | P. italicum | Kalimpong (WB) | Roy (1949) |
| 18 | Pestalotiopsis versicolor | Jabalpur (MP) | Agarwal & Hasiya (1974) |
| 19 | Phytopthora colocasiae | Bombay | Anonymous (1950) |
| 20 | Pullularia pullulans | Jodhpur (Rajasthan) | Panwar and Vyas (1973) |
| 21 | Rhizoctoria bataticola | Samrala (Punjab) | Parshar and Chohan (1966) |
| 22 | Rhizopus nigricans | Jabalpur<br>Lucknow | Ratnam & Nema (1967),<br>Sinha (1946) |
| 23 | Rosellinia bunodes | Poona<br>Bombay | Butler (1918),<br>Sydow & Sydow, (1916) |
| 24 | Stysanus monilioides | Darjeeling (WB) | Roy (1941) |
| 25 | Trichoderma lignorus | Kalimpong (WB)<br>Jabalpur (MP) | Roy, (1948)<br>Ratnam & Nema (1967) |
| 26 | Trichothecium roseum | Abohar (Punjab) | Cheema and Jayarajan, (1972) |

## 1. Blue Mould of Musambi—Sweet Orange

Blue mould rot of sweet orange is one of the most severe and destructive post-harvest known to occur throughout musambi growing areas. It causes heavy loss of fruits during transportation, storage and in the markets.

**Symptoms**

The infected fruits show watery patches on the fruit. The spot becomes brownish. The skin of the fruit can be easily peeled out. Such a lesions show, grey to whitish coloured fungal growth on affected region. The lesions increase gradually and show distinct zones around it. The sporulation I restricted only within the distinct zone i.e. on affected area. The mycelium of P. italicum does not extend much beyond the distinct zone around the lesions. Within 4-5 days of infection, the affected region start showing huge sporulation or blue mould occurs on fruit. In severe cases, complete fruit get covered by the growth of blue mold fungus and in very advanced stage of rot, the under laying tissue loose its turgidity.

**Cause**

Blue mould of musambi caused by Penicillium italicum reported by Roy (1949). The mycelium branched and hues. The conidiophores arise from the affected region of the fruit surface which is branched at the tip. The branching is dichotomous, conidia hyaline, globose or ovoid, unicellular, with basipetal growth pattern.

**Control**

1. Rao (1984) suggested Imazalil WP and EC for long term storage.
2. Chitzanidis, et. al. (1987) recommended fumigation for packing houses with formaldehyde.
3. Mishra (1989) suggested chemical impregnated wraps to control blue mould of kinnow fruits.
4. Careful collection and destruction of affected fruits can reduce intensity of blue mould.

## 2. Green Mould of Musambi—Sweet Orange

**Symptoms**

Disease can initiate on any part of the fruit. The occurrence and symptomatology and all other requirements of green mould development in the musambi fruit is similar as in blue mould disease except causal organism. The green mould of musambi fruits is caused by Penicillium digitatum Butler and Bisby (1931); Roy (1948);

Thom (1930). P. digitatum forms highly branched. pasty. wrinkled mycelium which produces green conidial mass in advanced stages of rot.

**Control**

1. As in blue mould disease of Musambi.
2. Ben. et al. (1992) suggested exposure of fruits to ultra violet rays for reduced susceptibility of fruits to P. digitatum.
3. Huang. et al. (1992) recommended Biocontrol agent Bacillus pumilus which can control P. digitatum.

## 3. Black Rot of Musambi—Sweet Orange

**Symptoms**

The black rot disease in Musambi start as a water soaked lesion. Lesion occurs on any part of the fruit. It increases in size with age. Later on, the big circular lesion gets depressed at the centre. In advanced stages, black mouldy growth of Aspergillus niger appears on the depressed lesion of the fruit. The lesion shows distinct zone around it, which is somewhat raised and water soaked. The whole fruit get rotted within 10-14 days. High humidity and temperature 260-300c is highly favourable for black rot development. In severe cases the skin of the fruit becomes soft and pulpy. The pathogen gains entry through the injured spaces.

**Cause**

Black rot of Musambi is caused by Aspergillus niger Van Tieghem. Shrivastava, et al. (1964); Shrivastva and Tandon (1968): Shrivastva and Tandon, (1969b); Roy (1948); Ratnam and Nema (1967). Conidiophores arise from the substratum and are smooth, septate or non-septate. The canidia are globose which are smooth or spinulose.

**Control**

1. Singh et al. (1985) recommended pre-harvest treatment of Sodium metabisulphite as protectant against A. niger.
2. It can be controlled by clean cultivation.
3. Dry aerated storehouse can reduce disease intensity.

4. Post-harvest dip treatment with fungicides like Benomyl 1500 ppm suggested by Bhargava and Singh (1975). It can control A. niger.
5. Dipping of fruits in hot water for reduction of A. niger rot recommended by Pathak and Shekhawat (1976).

## Post-harvest Rot Diseases of Grapes

**Table 9.2: Fungi causing rot disease of grapes**

| *Sl. No.* | *Fungus* | *Geography* | *Reference* |
|---|---|---|---|
| *1* | *2* | *3* | *4* |
| 01 | Cladosporium herbarium | Bombay Poona (MH) | Rao (1964f) |
| 02 | C. orysporum | Akola (MH) | Wangikar. et al. (1969 b) |
| 03 | Cochliobolus lunatus | Jonner (Rajasthan) | Goal, et al. (1971) |
| 04 | Curvularia pallescens | Allahabad (UP) | Jamaluddin and Tandon (1976) |
| 05 | Gloeosporium rufomaculans | Punjab | Devis (1931), Luthra (1932) |
| 06 | Pestalotia vicola | Bangalore (Karnataka) | Sohi & Prakash (1972) |
| 07 | Phytopthora nicotainae | Hessarghatta (Karnataka) | Sridhar, et al. (1975) |
| 08 | Gloeosporium ampelophagum | – | Sohi (1983) |
| 09 | Greeneria fuliginea | – | Prakash, et al. (1984) |
| 10 | Penicillium citrinum | Nainital | Tandon, et al. (1975) |
| 11 | Aspergillus niger | – | Singh and Kains (1983) |
| 12 | Glomerella cingulata | – | Daykin & Milholland (1984) |
| 13 | Botrytis cineria | – | – |

*(Table Contd...)*

| 1 | 2 | 3 | 4 |
|---|---|---|---|
| 14 | Pestalotia menezesiana | – | Mishra, et al. (1974) |
| 15 | Phomopsis viticola | – | Reddick (1909) |
| 16 | Periconia saraswatipurensis | – | Rai (1983) |

## 1. Rot of Grapes due to Gloeosporium sp

### Symptoms

On the berries, circular brown spots with dark brown margins develop leading to their shriveling and drying. The low temperature and high humidity are highly favourable for disease development.

### Cause

Pre-harvest rot of grapes in grape fields is caused by Gloeosporium ampelophagum pass.

### Control

1. All infected fruits should be pruned and destroyed by burning.
2. Use resistant varieties like Bharat and Hussaini.
3. Sohi and Sridhar (1972) recommended spraying of Bordeaux mixture immediately after pruning.

## 2. Bitter Rot of Grapes

### Symptoms

Fungus attacks unripe berries just near the peduncle. In severe cases, entire branches are infected. The berries drop down when the whole peduncle is infested. The affected berries are light brown to dark, full of dense acervuli but they do not shrivel. On young berries superficial circular brown spots develop. In advanced cases of infection, the discoloured are as coalesced and spread rapidly all over the fruit. Black acervuli of the fungus developed in the discoloured areas.

The causal agent is Greeneria fulliginea Scribner and Viala. (Prakash, et. al. 1974).

### 3. Post-harvest Rot of Grapes due to Periconia sp.

It is also known as soft rot disease.

#### Symptoms

The affected berries show water-soaked, slightly depressed spots which enlarge and becomes dark brown. White to pinkish mycelia of the causal agent along with fruiting bodies appeared on the centre of the diseased area and complete fruits get covered within 8-10 days of infection. The rotted fruits become pulpy and rotted fruits emit foul odour.

#### Cause

The disease is caused by Periconia saraswatipurensis (Rai, 1982).

#### Control

1. Rai (1982) recommended Vitanax 750 PPM for pre-harvest for treatment of grapes.
2. Careful handling can reduce disease intensity.
3. Storage at 5-100°C temperature can prevent soft rot by Periconia sp.

### 4. Post-harvest Rot of Grapes due to Phomopsis sp.

The disease is commonly known as dead arm disease. Lal and Arya (1982) reported such a dead arm disease from India.

#### Symptoms

In initial stages, the infected fruits shows small brown coloured dots which increases in size and becomes round which are encircled by dark brown margins. The affected tissue losses its turgidity and becomes pulpy. In severe cases, white mycelial grown appears on the fruit surface. The temperature between 25-28°C is highly favourable for the development of rot. The infected berries emit foul odour. The infected berries rot completely within 8-10 days.

#### Cause

The causal organism of dead arm disease of grapes is Phomopsis viticola Sacc. Reddick (1909); Costa Moria and Camara (1953); Seha (1961) and Cucuzza and Sall (1982) reported it from various parts of India. The pathogen produces dark black coloured, dot like fruiting bodies called Pycnidia.

**Control**

1. Remove infected berries from the lot to avoid spread of disease.
2. Injury to the ripe berries should be avoided to avoid infection.
3. Arya (1988a) a recommended 50 per cent extract of Eucalyptus and Aegle marmelos effective against dead arm disease of grapes.
4. Jaillowx, et al. (1987) recommended pre-harvest use of Fosetyl-Al plus Folpet for the control of dead arm disease.
5. Careful handling of fruits can reduce disease intensity.

## 5. Rot of Grapes due to Pestalotia sp.

**Symptoms**

Infection initiates at the top of the fruit. It increases and covers the upper part of the fruit within 3-4 days. The infected area becomes water-soaked which becomes light brown in colour. The fully nature fruits are more susceptible. The water soaked spots are irregular and slightly depressed. In severe cases, the spots get covered with acervuli. The infected fruits reduce market value. The injured fruits are more susceptible for infection.

**Cause**

The causal agent is Pestalotia menezesiana Bres & Torr. Mishra, et. al. (1974).

**Control**

1. Khanna and Chandra (1989) recommended fruit dip treatment in soap solution before storage.

## 6. Rot of Grapes due to Botrytis sp.

The pre-harvest infection to the fruits is also responsible for initiation of post-harvest rot of fruits. The rot caused by Botrytis sp. It is also known as grey mould disease. The grey mould rot of grape bunches occur before or after harvest during storage and

### Symptoms

The affected berries show soft smooth brown rot. In advanced stages the berries get enveloped by mycelial mat and grey spore masses. The injured berries are highly susceptible for grey mould disease. The shape of berries changes due to wet soft rot. The groups of affected rotted berries get mixed at this stage it is difficult to distinguish single affected berry.

### Cause

- Botrytis cineria Pers.

### Control

1. Removal and destruction of mummified fruits from grape stocks can reduce disease intensity during storage.
2. Well aerated dry godown restrict the growth of fungus during storage.
3. Nair (1985a) tried Captan & Benomyl against the disease.

## 7. Ripe Rot of Grapes

Shanmuganathan and Emmett (1985) reported ripe rot of grapes which is caused by Glomerella cingulata (Stonem) Spaulding and Schrenk. It is a widespread and destructive disease in grape growing fields. The young fruits get attacked and disease progresses until ripening of fruits (Daykin and Milholland, 1984). High humidity (100%) and moderate temperature is highly favourable for development of disease.

### Symptoms

The infected berries show small sunken spot of pale red to brown in colour. Gradually the spots increase in size, which shows concentric sings of dark coloured dot like acervuli. In severe cases, the skin of the infected berries gets cracked.

The affected berries degrade the quality and market value of the fruits.

### Cause

The disease is caused by Glomorella cingulata.

**Control**

1. Dayking and Milholland (1984) recommended applications of Benomyl, Captan, Manab after twice a month for bloom until harvest.
2. Remove and destruct infected berries to avoid secondary infection.

**8. Post-harvest Rot of Grapes due to Penicillium sp.**

Tandon, et al. (1975) found severe deterioration of grapes due to growth of Penicillium citrinum. The injured fruits are highly susceptible for the Penicillium rot disease. Infected fruits get covered with dull green coloured spores and hyphal branches.

**Cause**

Penicillium citrinum Thum.

**Control**

1. Tandon, et. al. (1977) recommended Bavistin (500 ppm) for the control of Penicillium rot of grapes.
2. Calyxin at 1000 ppm checks the Penicillium rot of grapes.
3. Captan (2000 ppm) effective against Penicillium rot of grapes.

**9. Post-harvest Rot of Grapes due to Aspergillus sp.**

Singh and Kainsa (1983) demonstrated the association of Aspergillus sp. on the cultivated plant during growing season. The Aspergillus sp. causes post-harvest rot of grape bunches during storage. Aspergillus niger is a common saprophytic fungus that grows on injured fruits during transportation and storage in Maharashtra.

**Cause**

Aspergillus niger Van Tiegh.

The pathogen A. niger is a severe pathogen, causes water soaked lesions on berries, which gradually increase and cover the complete berry. Destruction of berries due to A. niger is highest in presence of high humidity and moderate temperature. The infected fruits get covered with black canidial heads of fungus.

## Control

1. The systemic fungicides Bavistin & Ziride at 2000 ppm are effective against Aspergillus rot of grapes.
2. Captan (2000 ppm) restricts the Aspergillus rot of grapes.

# Bibliography


01. Anonymous (1950). *The Wealth of India*. Coun. Sci. & Indust. Res., Delhi, India, Vol. II.

02. Agarwal, G.P. and S.K. Hasiya (1974). A New Record of Pestalotiopsis Versicolor (Speg.) Sta. On Citrus Fruits. *Curr. Sci.*, 43: 50.

03. Agarwal, G.P. and S.K. Hasiya (1967). Alternaria Rots of Citrus Fruits. *Indian Phytopathology*, 20: 259-60.

04. Agarwal, G.P. and S.K. Hasiya (1961C). Fungi Causing Plant Diseases at Jabalpur (M.P.) — VII. *J. Indian Bet. Soc.*, 40: 542-47.

05. Anonymous (1974-85) *Studies on Diseases of Mango and their Control Rept. Pl. Pathol.* Central Mango Research Station Lucknow (INDIA).

06. Anonymous (1962a) Report Indian Agriculture Research Institute, Division of Mycology and Plant Pathology. New Delhi, *Agric. Res.*, 2: 8.

07. Anonymous (1950). List of Common Names of Indian Plant Diseases. *Indian J. Agric. Sci.*, 20; 107-142.

08. Ansar, M., Saleem, A. and Iqbal, A. 1994. Cause and Control of Guava Decline in Punjab Pakistan J. Phytopath. 6: 41-44.

09. Arya, A and Mathew D.S. 1991. Control of Phoma and Botryodiploidia Rots of Mango. *Geobios. New Reports* 10: 173-174.

10. Arya, A. (1988). Control of Phomopsis Fruit Rots of Grapes and Guava. *Indian Phytopath.* 41: 214-219.

11. Arya. A. (1982) Cultural & Pathological Studies of Certain Fungi Imperfecti. D. Phill. Thesis, Allahabad University. Allahabad, India.

12. Arya. A. (1988a) Control of Phomopsis Fruit Rots of Grapes and Guava. *Indian Phytopath*. 41 (2): 214-219.

13. Arya, A. Lal, B. Agarwal, R. and Srivastava, R.C. 1986. Some New Fruit Rot Diseases II: Symptomatology and Host Range. *Indian J. Mycol. Pl. Pathol.* 16(B): 265-269.

14. Badyal. K. and Sumbali. G. (1990) Post-harvest Diseases of Jujube. *J. Indian Bot, Soc.* 69: 189-190.

15. Bahtnagar, G.C. and N. Prasad (1966b) Studies on Fusarium Twig Disease of Lime (Citrus Aurantifolia Swingle). Indian *Phytopathology*, 19: 257-61.

16. Baker, R.E.D. (1938) Studies in the Pathogenicity of Tropical Fungi II Ann. Bot. N.S. 8: 919-931.

17. Bat, E.J. (1918) *Fungi and Diseases in Plants*. Thacker, Spink and Co., Calcutta.

18. Ben, Y.S.. Rodov, V., Kim, J.J. & Carmeli, S. (1992). Pre-formed & Induced Antifungal Materials of Citrus Fruits in Relation to the Enhancement of Decay Resistance by Heat and Ultraviolet Treatments. *J. Agri. Food Chemistry* 40: 1217-1221.

19. Bhargava, S.N. and Singh A.P. (1975). Aspergillus Rot of Mango-Its Control. *Indian J. Hort.* 32 (3-4): 190.

20. Bhargava, K.S. Gupta, S.D. (1957) Market Diseases of Fruits and Vegetables in Kumaon. 2. Rhizopus Rot of Plums (Prunus Communis). *Hortic. Adv.* 1: 65-67.

21. Bhargava, S.N. and Singh, A.P. (1974) Thiobendazole Storage of Guava Fruit. *Indian Phytopath*. 27: 613-617.

22. Bhargava, S.N. and Singh, A.P. 1975. Aspergillus Rot of Mango—Its Control. Indian J. Hort. 32(3-4): 190.

23. Bhargava, S.N. and Singh, A.P. 1975. Aspergillus rot of Mango: Its Control Indian J. Hortic. 32: 190.

24. Bhattacharya, B. and H.K. Baruah, (1953) Fungi of Assam. J. *Univ. Gauhati*, 4: 287-312.

25. Brain, P.W. Elson. G.W and Lowe. D. (1956) *Nature*. 178: 263.

26. Brown, E.A. and Hendrix, F.F. (1978) Effect of Certain Fungicides Sprayed during Apple Bloom on Fruit Set and Fruit Rot. *Plant Dis. Rep.* 62: 739-741.

27. Butler, E.J. (1914b) Rotting Pomegranates. *Agric. J. India*, 9: 205-206.

28. Butler, E.J. and G.R. Bisby (1931). The Fungi of India. Imp. Coun. of Ags. Res. *India Sci. Mono.* 1, XVIII, Calcutta.

29. Butler, E.J. (1914b) Rotting Pomegranates *Agric. J. India*, 9: 205-206.

30. Cambrink, J.C., Kotre, J.M., Wehner, F.C and Grobbelaar, C.J. (1986) Fungi Associated with Care Rot in Starking Apple in South Africa. *Phytophylactica* 17: 81-83.

31. Cash, E.K. and A.J. Watson, (1955) Some fungi on Orchidaceao. *Mycologia*, 47: 729-47.

32. Chakravarti, D.K. and D.N. Srivastava (1964) Stem and Rot of Mango and Orange Fruits Infected by Diploidia Natalensis Pole Evans. *Curr. Sci.*, 33: 285.

33. Chand, J.N. Kondal, M.R. and Agarwal, R.K. 1968. Epidemiology and Control of Bitter Rot of Apple caused by Gloeosporium Fructigenum Berk. *Indian Phytopath*. 21: 257-263.

34. Chandra and Tandon (1965c) Control of Leaf Spot of Pomegranate with Fungicides. *Sci. and Cult.*, 31: 536.

35. Chandra, S. and R.N. Tandon (1965c) Control of Leaf Spot of Pomegranate with Fungicides. *Sci. & Cult.*, 31: 536.

36. Chaube, H.S. (1984). Diseases of Papaya, *Indian Farmers Digest* 17(9): 13.

37. Chaube, S.H. (1984). Diseases of Fruit-mango. *Indian Farmers Digest*. 17 (1-2): 13.

38. Chaube, H.S. (1984). Diseases of Fruits and their Control-III Citrus. *Indian Farmers Digest*. 17(II): 7.

39. Chaudhry, S. (1950). Trans. Birt. *Mycol. Soci.* 33; 317-322.

40. Cheema, G.S and P.G., Dani, (1935) Report on the Export of the Mangoes to Europe in 1932 and 1933. *Bull. Dep. Ld. Rec. Agric.*, Bombay, 170: 1-31.

41. Cheema, S.S. and R. Jayarajan. 1972. A New Fruit Rot Disease of Sweet Orange caused by Trichothecium Roseum in Punjab. *Indian Phytopathology*, 25: 456-57.

42. Chitzanidis, A., Riethmacher, G. and Kranz., J. (1987). Penicillium Contamination and Effectiveness of Chemical Disinfection in Citrus Packing Houses in Greece. *Annales-de Institute-Phytopathologique-Benaki* 15: 109-119.

43. Ciferri, R. (1927) Rev. Patol. Veg. 17: 209.

44. Control of Mango Anthracnose by Fungicides. *Indian Phytopath.* 21: 212-216.

45. Costa Maria Da, E.A.P. and Camara, E. De. S. (1953) Species Aliquae Mycological Species II. *Protug. Acta. Biol.* 4: 162-176.

46. Cucuzza, J.D. and Sall, M.A. 1982. *California Agric.* 36 (2-3): 6-8.

47. Das Gupta, S.N. and R.S. Bhatt, (1946) Studies on the Diseases of Mangifera Indica L.J. *Indian bot. Soc.*, 25: 187-203.

48. Dastur, J.F. (1947) Report of the Head of the Division of Mycology and Plant Pathology. Sci, Rep. Agric. Res. Inst; New Delhi, 1946-47, pp. 109-117.

49. Davis, W.H. 1931. Anthracnose, Alternaria and Botrytis rot of the Snowberry Mycologia, 23: 177.

50. Daykin, M.F. and Milholland, R.D. 1984. Ripe Rot of Muscadine Grape caused by Colletotrichum gloeosporioides and its Control. *Phytopathology* 74: 710-714.

51. Dhingra, O.D. and M.N. Khare, 1971. A New Fruit Rot of Papaya Curr. Sci., 40: 612-13.

52. Dhingra, R & Mehrotra, R.S. (1980). A Few Unrecorded Post-harvest Diseases of Fruits and Vegetables. *Indian Phytopath.* 33: 475-76.

53. Garcha, H.S. and V. Singh, (1976). Penicillium Crustosum, A New Pathogen of Citrus Reticulata (Mandarin) from India. *Plant Disease Reptr.* 60: 252-54.

54. Garcha, H.S. and V. Singh, 1976. Penicillium Crustosum A New Pathogen of Citrus Reticulata (Mandaria) from India. Plant Disease Reptr. 60: 252-254.

55. Gerhardt (1942).

56. Goyal. J.P., B.G. Desai, L.G. Bhatnagar and V.N. Pathak. (1971) Fungal Collections from Rajasthan State of India. *Sydowia*. 25: 172-75.

57. Goyal, J.P., Desai, B.G. Bhatnagar, L.G. and Pathak, V.N. (1971) Fungal Collection from Rajasthan State of India, *Sydoria*, 26: 172-175.

58. Grewal. J.S. (1954) Cultural and Pathological Studies of Some Fungi Causing Diseases of Fruits. D. Phil. Thesis University of Allahabad.

59. Grove, W.B., (1935) *British Stem and Leaf Fungi (Ceolomycetes)*. Vol. II. Melanconiales. Cambridge, University Press.

60. Gupta, J.P. and Chatrath, M.S. (1973) Gamma Radiation for the Control of Post-harvest Fruit Rot of Guava (Psidium Guajava). *Indian Phytopath*. 26: 506-509.

61. Hasiya, S.K., (1962a) Additions to the Fungi of Jabalpur (M.P.) — I Mycopath. *Et Mycol. Appl.*, 18: 84-92.

62. Hingorani, M.K. Sharma, O.P. and Sohi, H.S. (1960) Studies on Blight Disease of Mango Caused by Macrophoma Mangiferae. *Indian Phytopath.* 13: 137-143.

63. Jailloux, F. Bugaret, Y. and Froidefand, G. (1987) Inhibition of Sporulation of Phomopsis Viticola Sacc. Cause of Dead Arm Disease of Vines by Fosetyl Al Under Field Conditions. *Crop. Protection* 6(3): 143-152.

64. Jamaluddin and Tandon, (1976) Some New Market Diseases of Vegetables and Fruits. *Indian Phytopath* 29: 74-75.

65. Jamaluddin, (1978). Cladosporium Rot of Fruits of Phyllanthus Emblica. *Proc. Nat. Acad. Sci. India*. 48(B): 62.

66. Jamaluddin, (1974) Studies on Fruit Rot of Lime Caused by Geotrichum Candidum. *Proc. Natl. Acad. Sci., India*, 44B: 250-52.

67. Jamaluddin, (1978) Cladosporium Rot of Fruits of Fruits of Phyllanthus Emblica. *Proc. Nat. Acad. Sci. India.* 48(B): 62.

68. Joshi, N.C. and K.P.T. Vishist, (1959) Fungi of Ajmer (Rajasthan) — IV. *Proc. Natl. Acad. Sci., India*, 2a: 147-50.

69. Kanitkar. U.K. and B.N. Uppal. (1939) Twig Blight and Fruit Rot of Mango. *Curr. Sci.*, 8: 470-71.

70. Kanwar, Z.S. and D.P. Thakur, (1973) Some New Fruit Rots of Pomegranate in Haryana. *Sci. & Cult.*, 274-76.

71. Kanwar, Z.S. and D.P. Thakur, (1973) Some New Fruit Rots of Pomegranate in Haryana. *Sci. & Cult.*, 39: 274-76.

72. Kapoor, I.J. (1970b) Occurrence of Curvularia Tuberculata Jain on Stored Fruits of Psidium Guava *L. Sydowia*, 24: 201-202.

73. Kapoor, I.J. and Tandon, R.N. (1970) A New Species of Macrophoma Causing Fruit Rot of Guava (Psidium Guajava) *Indian Phytopath.* 23: 122-125.

74. Kapoor, S.P. and Chohan, J.S. (1968) Ph. *Agric. Univ. J. Res.* 5: 56-57.

75. Kaushik, C.D.; Thakur, D.P. and Chand. J.N. (1972). Parasitism and Control of Pestalotia Psidii Causing Canerous Disease of Ripe Guava Fruits. *Indian Phytopath.* 25: 61-64.

76. Kehri, H.K. and Chandra, S. (1986) Control of Botryodiploidia Rot of Guava with Homeopathic Drug. *Nat. Acad. Sci. Letters* 9: 301-302.

77. Khanna, K.K. & Chandra, S. (1977). Control of Guava Fruit Rot Caused by Pestalotia Psidii with Homoeopathic drugs. *Plant Dis. Reptr.* 61: 362-366.

78. Khanna, K.K. and Chandra, S. (1976) Studies on Storage Diseases on Fruits and Vegetables. IV. Control of Guava Fruit Rot Caused by Pestalotia Psidii and C. Gloeosporioides with Aretan. *Curr. Sci*, 45: 270.

79. Khanna, K.K. and Chandra, S.S. (1978). A Homoeopathic Drug Controls Mango Fruit Rot Caused by Pestalotia Mangiferae Henn. *Experientia* 34: 1167-1168.

80. Khanna, K.K. and Chandra, (1975b). A New Disease Reporter, 59: 329-30.

81. Krishnainh, J., Satya Prasad, C.H. Singh, T.G. and Thirupathalah, V. (1985) Post-harvest Protection of Guava Fruits Using Decco Food Grade Fruit Coatings. *Indian Bot. Reporter* 4: 151-153.

82. Lal B. and Arya, A. (1982) A Soft Rot of Papaya. *Nat. Acad. Sci. Letters* 3(3): 73-74.

83. Lal, B. Rai, R.N. and Arya. A. (1979) Colletotrichum Rot of Papaya. *Nat. Acad. Sci. Letter* 3: 259-260.

84. Lal, B. and Arya, A. (1982). Three New Fusarial Rots of Papaya. *Nat. Acad. Sci. Letters* 3(3): 73-74.

85. Lal, B. and Rai, R.N. (1980) A New Soft Rot of 'Aonla' Caused b Phomopsis Phyllanthi Punith. And its Chemical Control. *Nat. Acad. Sci. Letters* 5(6); 183-186.

86. Lal, B. Rai, R.N. Arya, A. and Tewari, D.K. (1980) A New Soft Rot of Guava *Nat. Acad. Sci. Letters* 3: 259-260.

87. Lal, B. Rai, R.N. Arya, A. and Tewari, D.K. 1982. Chemical Control of Thielaviopsis Rots of Gurav. *Indian J. Hort.* 39: 293-294.

88. Lal, B. Rai. R.N. Arya, A. and Tewari, D.K. 1980. A New Soft Rot of Guava Nat. Acad. Sci. Letters 3: 259-260.

89. Lal, B. Tewari, D.K. Agarwal R. and Srivastava, R.C. (1984) Some New Host Records of Ulocladium Chartarum (Prreuss) Simmons. *Proc. Nat. Acad. Sci. India* 54(B): 129.

90. Laxminarayana, P. and Reddy, S.M. (1975) A New Post-harvest Disease of Mango. *Indian Phytopath.* 28(4): 529-530.

91. Luthra, J.C., (1932) Some Fungal Diseases of Farm Crops Recently Discovered in the Punjab. *Int. Bull. Plant. Prot.*, 5: M 188; and 6: 182 M.

92. Majumdar, V.L. and Pathak, V.N. (1991) Effect of Hot Water Treatment on Post-harvest Disease of Guava Fruits. *Acta Botanical India*. 19: 79-80.

93. Mathur, R.L.; R.N.S. Tyagi, and J.P. Agnihotri (1962). Fungi—Cole Parasites from Rajasthan *Sci. & Cult.*, 28: 488.

94. Mc Rae. 1924. Economic Botany Part III. Mycology Annual Report Board Scientific Advice. India 1922-23; 31-35.

95. Mc Rae, W. (1924). Economic Botany Part III. Mycology. Ann. Rept. Board Scientific Advice, India, 1922-23; 31-35.

96. Mehrotra. B.S and M.D. Mehrotra (1963) A Morphological and Physiological Study of Gilberella in India. *Mycologia*, 55: 582-94.

97. Mehta, O.R. (1940) Stem and Rot and Soft Rot of Pineapple in the United Province. *Curr. Sci.*, 9:30.

98. Mishra, B.P. (1989). A Note on Control of Blue Mould of Kinnow Fruits Caused by Penicillium Italicum Through Diphenyl Wrappers. Haryana. *J. Hort. Sci.* 18(1-2): 65-66.

99. Mishra, B. Prakash, Om, Misra, A.P. (1974) Pestalotia Menezesiana on Grape Berries from India. *Indian Phytopath* 27: 257-258.

100. Mitter, J.H. and R.N. Tandon, (1930a) The Fungus Flora of Allahabad. *J. Indian Bot. Soc.*, 9: 197.

101. Mohanty. U.N., 1948. Studies on Indian Aspergilli. *Indian Phytopathology*, 1: 55-56..

102. Nair, N.G. (1985a) The Fungi Associated with Bunch Rot of Grapes in the Hunter Valley. *Anst. Jour. Agri. Res.* 36: 435-442.

103. Pandey, R.S. Khati, D.V.S. Shukla, D.N. and Bhargava, S.N. (1980) A New Phoma Rot of Phyllanthus Emblica. *Indian Phytopath.* 33: 491.

104. Pandey, R.S. Dwivedi, D.K., Shukla, D.N. and Bhargava, S.N. (1980) Two New Fungicides for the Control of Aspergillus Rot of Mango. *Nat. Acad. Sci. Letters* 3: 263-264.

105. Panwar, K.S. and N.L. Vyas, (1973) A Post-Harvest Fruit Rot of Citrus Reticulata Blanco. *Curr. Sci.*, 42: 217-18.

106. Panwar, K.S and N.L. Vyas (1974). Cladosporium Oxysporium Causing Fruit Rots of Punica Granatum. Zizyphus Jujube and Capsicum Amunm. *Indian Phytopath.* 27: 121-22.

107. Parashar, R.D. and J.S. Chohan. (1966) New Record of Fruit Rot of Mandarin Orange (Citrus Reticulata) caused by Rhizoctoria Bataticola (Taub.) Butler. *Indian Phytopathology*, 19: 315-16.

108. Patel. K.D. and Pathak, U.N. (1993) Incidence of Guava Fruit Rots and Losses due to Rhizopus and Botryodiploidia in Udaipur and Ahmedabad Markets. *Indian J. Mycol. Plant Pathol.* 23: 273-277.

109. Patel, K.D. and Pathak, V.N. (1993) Influence of Guava Fruit Rots and Losses due to Rhizopus and Botryodiploidia in Udaipur and Ahmedabad Markets. *Indian Mycol. Plant Patho.* 23: 273-277.

110. Patel. K.D. and Pathak, V.N. 1995. Development of Botryodiplodia Rots of Guava Fruits in Relation to Temperature and Humidity. *Indian Phytopath.* 48: 86-89.

111. Patel, M.K. and Padhye, Y.A. 1948. Bacterial Soft Rot of Mango in Bombay. *Indian Phytopath.* 1: 127-128.

112. Patel, M.K., M.N. Kamat and V.P. Bhinde, 1949. Fungi of Bombay. Suppl. I.. *Indian Phytopathology*, 2: 142-55.

113. Pathak, U.N. and Shekhawat, P.S. (1976) Efficacy of Some Fungicides and Hot Water in Control of Anthracnose and Aspergillus Rot of Mango Fruits. *Indian Phytopath.* 37: 682-683.

114. Pathak, V.N. Goyal, J.P. and Bhatnagar, L.G. (1976). Effect of Chemials and Hot Water Treatment on Fusarium and Rhizopus Rots of Papaya'. *Indian Phytopath.* 29(2): 210-211.

115. Pathak, V.N., Goyal, J.P. and Sharma, H.C. (1971) Screening Trials for Control of Diplodia and Rhizopus Rots of Mango Fruits. *Plant Dis. Rep.* 55: 752.

116. Prakash, O. and Raoof, M.A. (1985) Die Back Disease of Mango and its Control. Second Int. Sym. Mango, Bangalore, 50 PP.

117. Prakash, O. and Singh, V.N. 1976. A New Diseases of Mango. Fruit Res. Workshop. Hyderabad. May 24-28.

118. Prakash, O. and Srivastava, K.C. (1987) Mango Diseases and their Management—A World Review. Today & Tomorrow's Print. And Publ. New Delhi, 175.

119. Prakash, O. Mishra, B. and Mishra, A.P. (1974). Greeneria Fulinea. Scibner and Viola Causing Bitter Rot of Grapes. *Indian Phytopath.* 27: 605-606.

120. Prasad, S.S. and Verma, R.A.B. (1970) Fungal Diseases of Papaya Fruit in Bihar. *Indian Phytopath.* 23: 722-724.

121. Rai, R.N. (1982) Pathological & Physiological Studies of Certain Fungi Causing Fruit Rot Disease. D. Phil. Thesis University of Allahabad. 217 pp.

122. Rai, R.N. Lal. B. and Arya, A. (1982a). Some New Fruit Rot Diseases. *Indian J. Mycol. Pl. Pathol.* 12: 264-266.

123. Raina, G.L., Bedi, P.S. and Dutt, S. (1971) Occurrence of Core Rots of Apple in Nature in the Kullu Valley of Himachal Pradesh, *India. Plant Dise. Rep.* 55: 283-284. 138. Rao (1984).

124. Rao, V.G. (1964 f) Some New Market and Storage Diseases of Fruits and Vegetables in Bombay, Maharashtra. *Mycopath. Et Mycol. Appl.*, 23: 297-310.

125. Rao, V.G. (1965 a) Some New Records of Market and Storage Diseases of Vegetables in Bombay, Maharashtra, *Mycopath. Et. Mycol. Appl.*, 27: 48-59.

126. Rao, V.G. 1966b. An Account of the Market and Storage Diseases of Fruits and Vegetables in Bombay. Maharashtra. *Mycopath. Et. Mycol. Appl.*, 28: 165-76.

127. Rath, G.C. and Mohanan, M.K. (1986) Fungi Inciting Fruit Rot of Mango. *Indian Phytopath.* 39(4): 612-613.

128. Ratnam, C.V. and K.G. Neema, (1967) Studies on Market Diseases of Fruits & Vegetables. *The Andhra Agri. J.*, 14; 60-65.

129. Reddick, D. (1909). Necdrosis of Grapevine. *Cornell Univ. Agr. Expt. Sta. Bull.* 263: 323-342.

130. Roy, A.K. (1948). Fungi of Bental. *Bot. Soc. Bengal* (Special Number).

132. Roy, A.K. (1949) Rungi of Bengal. Bot. Soc. Bengal, 2: 134-77.

133. Roy, A.K. (1965 b) Additions to the Fungus Flora of Assam. I. Indian Phytopathology, 18: 327-55.

134. Roy, T.C. (1941) A New Pathogen Causing Decay of Orange Fruits (Citrus Crysocarpa Lush.) *Sci. & Cult.*, 6: 551.

135. Roy, T.C. (1948) Fungi of Bengal. *Bull. Bot. Soc. Bengal*, 2: 134-77.

136. Roy, T.C. (1949) Fungi of Bengal. Bot. Soc. Bengal (Special Number).

137. Saha, J.C. (1945) Studies in Rots of Indian Fruits. I. Occurrence of Latent and Superficial Infections. *Indian J. Agric. Sci.*, 15: 332-338.

138. Sattar, A. and Malik, S.A. (1939) Some Studies on Anthracnose of Mango Caused by Glomerella Cingulata (Stonem). Spauld. Sch. Colletotrichum Gloeosporioides Penz. *Indian Jour. Agric. Sci.* 1: 511-521.

139. Setty, K.G.H., (1959) Blue Mould of Aonla (Phyllanthus Emblica L.). *Curr. Sci.*, 28: 208.

140. Setty, K.G.H., (1959) Blue Mould of Aonla (Phyllanthus Emblica L.). *Curr. Sci.*, 28: 208.

141. Shankhapal, K.V. (1976) Candida Rot of Mandarin Oranges in India. *Plant Disease Reptr.* 60: 237-38.

142. Shanmuganathan, N. and Emmett. R. (1985-86) Disease Problems Associated with Grape Production in the tropics and Sub-tropics. *Int. Rev. Trop. Pl. Path* 2 (Eds. S.P. Raychandhuri and J.P. Verma) 141-173.

143. Sharma, B.B. and J.P. Tewari, (1969) Epichloe Cinerea on Sporobolus Indicus from India. Mycopath, Et Mycol. Appl; B7: 221-24

144. Sharma, J.K.; Singh, J.P. and Chand, J.M. (1984). Chemical Control of Anthracnose of Guava Causal by Glomerella Cingulata Haryana. *Agric. Univ. J. Res.* 13: 325-326.

145. Sharma, N.D., R. Singh and A.C. Jain, (1981) Some New Fungi Recorded on Pineapple. *Indian Phytopathology*, 34-245.

146. Shinde, P.A. and M.N. Asalmol. (1968-69) Two Serious Diseases of Santra in Vidarbha. Nagpur. *Agri. Coll. Mag.*, 41: 69-72.

147. Shukla, D.N., Bhargava, S.N. and Singh, N.K. (1978) A Note on Stalk Rots of Papaya on Fruits. *Indian J. Hort.* B 5 (3): 282-283.

148. Siddiqui, M.R. (1963) Taxonomy and Pathogenicity of the Genus alternaria with Special Reference to India Species. *J. Indian Bot. Soc.*, 42: 260-72.

149. Simmonds. J.H. (1965) A Study of the Species of Colletotrichum Causing Ripe Fruit Rots in *Queensland. Queensland J. Agric. And Ani. Sci.* 32: 437-459.

150. Singh et. al. (1985).

151. Singh, A.P. & Bhargava, S.N. (1977). Benlate As An Effective Post-harvest Fungicide for Guava Fruits. *Indian J. Hort.* 34: 309-312.

152. Singh, J.P. and Krinsa, R.L. (1983). Microbial Flora of Grapes in Relation to Storage and Spoilage. *Indian Phytopath* 36(1): 72-76.

153. Singh, J.P. Sharma, Sushil and Yamadagni, R. (1985) Control of Post-harvest Black Mould of Grapes. *Indian Phytopath.* 38(3) 531-532.

154. Singh, R.S. and J.S. Chohan (1972a). A New Fruit Rot Disease of Pomegranate. *Curr. Sci.*, 41: 651.

155. Singh, V.B. (1943b) Some Diseases of Fruits and Fruit Trees in Kumaon—*LICAR Misc. Bull.*, 51-16.

156. Singh, A.K., and K.C. Basu Chaudhary, 1974. Ceratocystis Soft Rot of Sweet Orange Curr. Sci., 43: 726-27.

157. Sinha, S. (1946). On Decay of Certain Fruits in Storage. Proc. Indian Acad. Sci., 24B: 198-205.

158. Smith, W.L. and Anderson, R.E. (1975) Decay Control of Peaches and Nectarines During and After Controlled Atmosphere and Air Storage. *J. American Soc. Hortic. Sci.* 100: 84-86.

159. Sohi, (1975) Anthracnose in Tropical Fruit Adv. *Mycol. Plant Pathol.* 193-204.

160. Sohi, H.S. (1983). Disease of Tropical and Sub-tropical Fruits and their Control. *Recent Advances in Plant Pathology* (eds. Akhtar Husain, B.P. Sing, V.P. Agnihotri and Kisan Singh) Print House India Lucknow, 521 pp.

161. Sohi, H.S. and O. Prakash, 1972. New Records of Fungal Fungi from India. *Indian Phytopath.* 22: 410-12.

162. Sohi, H.S. and Sridhar, T.S. (1972). *Indian J. Hort.* 28: 116.

163. Sohi, H.S. and Sokhi, S.S. and Tiwari, R.P. (1973). Studies on the Storage Rot of Mango Caused by Colletotrichum Gloeosporioides Penz. *Phytopathol. Medit.* 12: 114-116.

164. Solangi, G.P. and Malik, M.S.S. (1971) Studies on Physiological Behaviour of Colletotrichum Dematium (Pers. Ex Fr.) Grove, Causing Anthracnose of Papaya Fruit. *J. of Agr. Res. Lahore* 9(1): 50-61.

165. Spalding, D.H. and Reeder, W.E. (1972). Post-harvest Disorders of Mangoes as Affected by Fungicides and Heat Treatment. *Plant Dis. Reptr.* 59: 751-753.

166. Sridhar, T.S. 1974. Evaluation of Fungicides Against Rhizopus sp. Causing Soft Rot of Fruits. *Hindustan Antibiotic Bull.* 17: 31-34.

167. Sridhar, T.S., 1975. Black Rot of Pineapple—A New Record from South India. *Curr. Sci.*, 44: 869.

168. Sridhar, T.S., B.A., Ullasa and H.S. Sohi, 1975. Occurrence of a New Disease on Grape Seedlings Caused by Phytopthora Nicotianae Var. Parasitica (Dastur) Water House from India. *Curr. Sci.*, 44: 406.

169. Srivastava, M.P. and R.N. Tandon (1971) Aspergillus Rots of Pomegranate. *Indian Phytopath*, 24: 172.

170. Srivastava, M.P. (1966). Cultural and Pathological Studies of Certain Fungi Causing Post-harvest Disease of Some Fruits. D. Phil. Thesis, Allahabad Univ., Allahabad, India 299 pp.

171. Srivastava, M.P. and R.N. Tandon (1968). Some Storage Diseases of Fruits. *Curr. Sci.*, 37; 292.

172. Srivastava, M.P. and R.N. Tandon (1969b). Some Storage Diseases of Orange. *Indian Phytopathology*, 22: 124.

173. Srivastava, M.P. and R.N. Tandon, (1969b). Some Storage Diseases of Orange. *Indian Phytopathology*, 22: 124.

174. Srivastava, M.P. and R.N. Tandon. 1968. Some Storage Disease of Fruits. *Curr. Sci.*, 37: 292.

175. Srivastava, M.P. and Tandon, R.N. Bhargava, S.N. and Ghosh, A.K. (1965). Studies on Fungal Diseases of Some Tropical Fruits III. Some Post-harvest Diseases of Mango. *Proc. Nat. Acad. Sci. India* 35B: 69-75.

176. Srivastava, M.P. and Tandon, R.N. Bhargava, S.N. and Ghosh, A.K. (1965) Studies on Fungal Diseases of Some Tropical Fruits III. Some Post-harvest Diseases of Mango. *Proc. Nat. Acad. Sci. India*, 35B: 69-75.

177. Srivastava, M.P. and Tandon, R.N. Bilgrami, K.S. and Ghosh, A.K. (1964a) Studies on Fungal Diseases of Some Trgrical Fruits and Fruits Trees. *Phytopath. Z.* 50(3); 250-261.

178. Srivastava, M.P., Chandra, S. and Tandon, R.N. (1946b) Post-harvest Diseases of Some Fruits & Vegetables *Proc. Nat. Acad. Sci. India* 34(4): 339-342.

179. Srivastava, M.P., R.N. Tandon, K.S. Bilgrami and A.K. Ghosh, (1964) Studies on Fungal Diseases of Some Tropical Fruits, I. A List of Fungi Isolated from Fruits and Fruit Tree Phytopathology Z., 50: 250-61.

180. Srivastava, M.P., R.N. Tandon, S.N. Bhargava and A.K. Ghosh (1964). Studies on Fungal Diseases of Some Tropical Fruits, I.A. List of Fungi Isolated from Fruits and Fruit tree. Phytopathology Z., 50: 250-61.

181. Srivastava, M.P., R.N. Tandon, S.N. Bhargava and A.K. Ghosh (1966) Studies on Fungal Diseases of Some Tropical Fruits—IV. Some New Fungi. *Mycopath. Et. Mycol. Appl.*, 30: 203-208.

182. Srivastava, M.P., S. Chandra and R.N. Tandon, (1964). Post-harvest Diseases of Some Fruits and Vegetables. *Proc. Natl. Acad. Sci.*, 34B: 339-42.

183. Srivastava, O.P. (1968) Soft Rot of Desi Mango Fruit and the Pathogenicity of the Isolated Microorganisms. *J. Ind. Bot Soc.* 47: 328-329.

184. Srivastava, R.C. Arora, S., Tewari, D.K. and Lal, B. (1986) Phoma Rot of Phyllanthus Emblica L. *Geobois New Reports* 5: 195-196.

185. Sydow, H. and P. Sydow (1916) No. XIV, *Ann. Mycol.*, 14: 256-61.

186. Tandon, I.N. and Singh, B.B. (1968). Control of Mango Anthracnose by Fungicides. *Indian Phytopath.* 21: 212-216.

187. Tandon, M.P. Jamauddin and Bhargava, V. (1975 a) Some New Fruit Rot Diseases. *Indian Phytopath* 28(4): 570-572.

188. Tandon, M.P., V. Bhargava and Jamaluddin, 1975. Some New Fruits Rot Diseases. *Curr. Sci.*, 44: 708.

189. Tandon, R.N. (1967) Final Technical Report PL-480 Scheme (FG-IN-133) University of Allahabad.

190. Tandon, R.N. 1969. Final Technical Report PL-480 Scheme (FG-IN-133). University of Allahabad.

191. Tandon, R.N. and S.N. Bhargava, (1962) Botryodiploidia Rot of Pineapple (Ananas Comosus Men.) *Curr. Sci.*, 31: 344-45.

192. Tandon, R.N. and Verma, A. (1964). Some New Storage Diseases of Fruits and Vegetables. *Curr. Sci.*, 33: 625-627.

193. 4ies on Fungal Diseases of Some Tropical Fruits (Abs). *34th Ann. Sess. of Nat. Acad. Sci. India.* 58-59p.

194. Tewari, D.K. Srivastava, R.C., Katiyar, W. Arora, S. and Lal, B. (1988). Post-harvest Diseases of Fruits. *Proc. Nat. Acad. Sci. India* 58(B): 345-346.

195. Tewari, D.K., Srivastava, R.C. Katiyar, N. and Lal, B. (1988) Chemical Control of Thielaviopsis Rots of Papaya. *Indian Phytopath.* 41: 491-492.

196. Thakur, D.P. (1972) A New Host for Rhizopus Stolonifer, *Indian Phytopath.* 25: 158-60.

197. Thakur, D.P. (1972). Factors Influencing Storage Rot of Certain Fruits and Vegetables Caused by Three Species of Rhizopus, *Indian Phytopath.* 25 (3): 354-358.

198. Thakur, D.P. and Chenulu, V.V. (1970) Chemical Control of Soft Rot of Apple and Mango Fruits Caused by Rhizopus Arrhizus *Indian Phytopath.* 23(1): 58-61.

199. Thakur, D.P. and Chenulu, V.V. (1966). Survey of Delhi Market for Fungal Diseases of Fruits and Vegetables. Plant Disease Problem. Proc. Int. Sym. On Plant Pathology, Indian Phytopath. Soc. New Delhi pp. 308-315.

200. Thakur, D.P. and Chenulu, V.V. (1970) Chemical Control of Soft Rot of Apple and Mango Fruits Caused by Rhizopus Arrhizus. *Indian Phytopathol.* 23: 58-61.

201. Thind, K.S. and G.S. Rawla, (1961b). A Coletotrichum Sp. On Citrus. *Indian Phytopathology*; 14: 26-29.

202. Thom, C. 1930. *The Penicillia.* The Wiliams & Wikins Co., Baltimore, U.S.A.

203. Thom, C. and K.B. Raper, 1945. *A Mannual of the Aspergilli.* The Williams & Wilkins Co., Baltimore, U.S.A.

204. Thom, C., *The Penicillia.* The Williams and Wilkins Co., Baltimore, U.S.A.

205. Tilak, S.T. and R. Rao (1970). *Second Supplement to the Fungi of India*, Maharashtra (Marathwada University).

206. Ullasa, B.A. and Rawel, R.D. (1975) Occurrence of New Post-harvest Disease of Mango due to Pestalotia Glandicola (Abs.) Second Int. Symp. on Mango. Bangalore, (India) 64p.

207. Uppal, B.N. and M.K. Patel, and M.N. Kamat, (1935) *The Fungi of Bombay.* VIII. (Private Publication, pp. 1-56).

208. Uppal, B.N., M.K. Patel and M.N. Kamar, (1952) Black Spot of Mango Fruits. *Indian Phytopathology*, 5: 44-46.

209. Uppal, B.W. and M.N. Kamat, (1933) India; Diseases in the Bombay Presidency. *Int. Bull. Pl. Prot.* 7: M103 and M 746.

210. Viegas, A.P. (1946) Some Fungi of Brazil (*S. Paulo) Bragantia 6: 1-37.

211. Vir, D. and R. Sharma, (1965) A Note of Mango Fruit Rots in Storage. Indian Phytopathology, 18: 390-91.

212. Vyas, N.L. (1976) A New Post-harvest Disease of Pomegranate in India. *Curr. Sci.*, 45: 76.

213. Wangikar, P.D., J.G. Raut, and N. Gopal Krishna, (1969 b) Cladosporium Oxysporium Causing Mould on Grape Berries and Leaves. *Indian Phytopath.* 22: 404-5.

214. Wangikar, P.D. and Rout, J.G. (1972). Notes on Some Plant Diseases Round About Akola. Punjab Rao Krishi Vidyapeeth Res. J. 1(1): 139-140.

215. Wangikar, P.D., J.G. Rent, and N. Gopal Krishna, (1969b) Cladosporium Oxyporium Causing mould on Grape berries and Leaves. *Indian Phytopath.* 22: 404-05.

216. Wardlaw, C.W. and Leonord, E.R. (1936). The Storage of West Indies Mangoes. *Mem Low. Temp. Res. Sta.* 2: 47.

217. Wilson, D.M. and Nuovo, G.L. (1973). Appl. Microbial. 26: 124-125.

# Index